WALKING IN A WITCHY WONDERLAND

JULIETTE CROSS

Cover Art by Jennifer Zemanek.

For my beloved son, Jacob.
Hoping you find your JJ or Charlie or Thomas.
Someone to love and cherish the brilliant, kind-hearted man that you are.

BEWITCH YOU A MERRY CHRISTMAS

Timeline: Takes place in December immediately following* **Wolf Gone Wild.

CHAPTER 1

~EVIE~

"You want me to do what now?"

I stared at the thirtyish man in his well-starched shirt and fancy tie swallowing up the two-top table with his muscular frame. He pointed to his nose.

"I look like fucking Rudolph!"

He really did. His nose was puffy as if he had a cold, but much ruddier than someone with a sniffle. And it had a nice sheen on the bulbous tip like a glossy bowling ball. A shame, that. Because he'd be very good looking if it weren't for his ridiculously red and swollen nose.

"It could just be a bad cold. Why do you think this is

a curse?" I asked calmly, flicking my gaze to my sister Violet. She stood behind the bar near us, chin in both hands, elbows on the counter, her Poinsettia-red dyed hair falling around her pale face, watching us with unabashed delight.

It was always my first instinct to be skeptical when someone came in, swearing that a curse had been put on them. Only about twenty-five percent of the complainants who come to me actually had a witch's hex put on them.

"That's not all," he blustered.

He glanced around then jumped up and stomped over to the Christmas tree next to our small stage for live entertainment. He grabbed an ornament off the tree, then huffed back over to me. Thankfully, it was four o'clock, our daytime lull for customers. However, a man reading his paper and drinking a Witch's Brew longneck did pause to watch the angry guy plucking something off our Christmas tree before storming back across the room.

Mr. Romano sat back down, the chair creaking beneath his weight. He was over six feet tall with a thick build. But I didn't get any menacing vibes from him. They were all directed at the witch he claimed put the hex on him. She lived in the other half of the duplex building he rented.

He slapped the ornament on the table. It was a metal

angel with a skirt made into a bell. He pointed at the offending ornament, squinting his eyes like a snake ready to strike.

"Ring that bell," he commanded gruffly.

"I'm sorry?"

"Ring it."

Arching a brow at his aggressiveness, I lifted the obviously offensive angel ornament and gave it a little tinkling ring. His scowling face suddenly transformed into a comical doll-like expression then he said in a girly voice, "Every time a bell rings, an angel gets its wings."

Violet burst into cackling laughter behind me. I shot her a death-glare then returned my steady gaze to Mr. Romano whose expression hardened back into the deep scowl he'd been wearing since he stepped into the Cauldron ten minutes ago. I reached for the bell again.

"Please don't do it," he begged, expression tight and grim. "Every time I hear a bell, I'm compelled to say that damn line from that old black and white Gary Cooper Christmas movie.

I looked over at Violet. "Gary Cooper Christmas movie?"

My sister rolled her eyes. "He means Jimmy Stewart. *It's a Wonderful Life.*"

Okay, now I had to admit this was looking like a curse.

"Please ring it again," pleaded Violet, barely smothering her wicked glee.

I shot her another warning glare then returned my attention to Mr. Romano. "Is there anything else?"

He scratched his jaw where his day-old scruff was morphing into a beard. I wasn't sure if the hair growth was intentional or if this curse just had him so off-balanced he'd given up on regular hygiene. He was dressed impeccably, but the rest of him looked awful.

He mumbled something I didn't quite hear.

"What was that?"

"Wish me a Merry you-know-what." He gave a flourish of his fingers for me to fill in the blank.

Before I could even open my mouth, Violet belted out, "Merry Christmas!"

Mr. Romano slammed a fast on the table, his brows slanted into an angry V, then growled dramatically, "*Bah* humbug!"

Violet fell into a fit of laughter, drawing our bartender JJ's attention, from where he was at the other end of the bar, talking to his one lone customer. Actually, the well-dressed gentleman was leaning in, gaze riveted on JJ. Looked like more than talking was going on. Good for JJ. He had been in a dating dry spell and needed to venture out there again. Maybe it was just because I was crazy happy and in love, but I wanted everyone to find themselves a Mateo. Not *my* Mateo, mind you, but their own version of my amazing, gorgeous, sexy-as-hell, werewolf boyfriend.

Violet choked on her own spit as she cackled, drawing me back to the present. Poor Mr. Romano looked appropriately humiliated. A sizzling charge in the air tingled along my skin, telling me that magic simmered in the room. I didn't need to even "check" to see if this was a curse, but I figured I'd better go through the motions anyway. It would look more legit if he saw me behaving a little more woo-woo, like a witch who knew what she was doing. Besides, I needed something simple after my last job. That one had been a doozy. The only good thing about the last one was that it dropped Mateo into my lap. And into my bed, thank the heavens.

"Hold out your hand, Mr. Romano."

He held out one of his giant paws, well-manicured, but broad with a thick, silver ring around his index finger. I took hold of him and closed my eyes. Within a millisecond, the electric charge of magic sizzled straight through my hand and shot up my arm, giving me a little shiver. I suppressed the smile, because the witch behind the hex was a benevolent one. Tracings of her personality mingled with the magic, telling me all I needed to know. As if I wasn't sure of it already, this hex was the hexer's idea of a joke. Still, he was hiring me to break it, and I would. First things first.

"Oh, I see," I said, knitting my brow, putting on a grave face.

"What?" he asked eagerly. "What do you see?"

Opening my eyes, I let go of his hand and straightened my posture. "You're right. Definitely a curse. However, I'll need to come to your duplex to break it."

He ground out a few profane words under his breath, balling his meaty hand into a fist. "Why not now?"

"I need to be where you were when the hex was placed on you."

Totally a lie. It didn't matter at all. I just needed to meet the witch responsible, face-to-face.

He grumbled something under his breath. I swear, if this guy had any magic of his own, I'd think he was a werewolf with all the snarling noises he was making.

"I've got a meeting uptown in an hour, then a business dinner." He pushed both hands through his hair, leaning back and linking his fingers behind his neck, his brown-eyed gaze focused on the ceiling. "I don't think I can make it through without incident," he said more to himself.

Damn, this guy really was suffering. "What time is your next meeting over?"

Gaze leveling on me with a heavy exhale, he mumbled, "Four thirty. I should already be on my way."

"And your dinner?"

"Eight. In Metairie."

"No problem." I glanced at Violet who was still completely riveted to my little business transaction. "I'll meet you at your place at six-thirty, break the curse, and be gone within half an hour. Plenty of time for you to get to your business dinner."

"You can do it that quick?"

This curse would take me about thirty seconds to unlock and release. But I didn't tell him that. I needed some time to find out what this was really all about and keep it from happening again. His little Christmas hex was created with benign magic. But if I didn't get to the bottom of why she hexed him in the first place, it could escalate to something more sinister if she was a vindictive kind of person.

That was one thing no one realized about a hex-breaker's job. Removing the hex was only one part. I had to get to the root of why it had been put on the hexee in the first place. I was sort of a problem-solver or conflict mediator to make sure both parties were at peace with each other by the time it was said and done.

My sisters and I, the Savoie Sisters as our coven was known, played the part of law enforcers and peace-keepers among the supernaturals of New Orleans. We each held a unique magical gift to tackle different problems among our fellow witches, the vampires, the werewolves, and the elusive grim reapers. Actually, we'd never had to intervene with any grim that I'd ever known. But that wasn't unusual. They kept to themselves and stayed out of trouble. Or they covered their tracks too well when they did get into a mess.

The vampires tended to attract trouble, but their beauty and magnetism wasn't their fault. The werewolves tended to have huge blowouts of violence that was quelled quickly or they stayed off the radar entirely. Like my darling Mateo. Until he was completely and totally on my radar.

Surprisingly, it was the other witches who seemed to cause the most mischief. Like whoever had put this hex on Marcus Romano. So I had to intervene and do more than remove the hex. I'd confront her and make sure all was well and that this wasn't going to escalate into some sort of turf war between the witch and her dominant, overbearing neighbor. Because with the way he was trying to control our short meeting, when he should at least attempt to be placating since he needed my help, told me a lot about Mr. Romano. He was a man used to getting what he wanted and accustomed to stomping over others to get it.

"Fine, fine," he grumbled, pulling out a business card and scribbling an address on the back. Then he stuck out his ham-sized hand for me to shake. "I'll see you at six-thirty. On the dot." He arched a commanding brow at me, his voice going gruff. I wanted to laugh at his attempt to intimidate me, if that's what this was. He didn't know I'd wrestled with the most dominant alpha of them all and won—Mateo's wolf. Actually, that was what his wolf called himself. Alpha. He had a voice of his own inside Mateo's head. If his self-appointed name didn't fit him like a glove, it would be laughable. But there was little about Mateo's wolf that made me laugh. Moan? Melt? Shiver? Scream his name? Yeah. But not laugh.

"On the dot." I shook Mr. Romano's hand. "I'm curious. How'd you know to come to me?"

Few humans knew that supernaturals lived amongst them, that magic was real. Those who did know pretended they didn't, because who would believe them, right?

He stood from the table. "I've done some business with Ruben Dubois."

"Ahh." I nodded.

That was all the explanation needed. If he'd done business with the head of the vampire coven in New Orleans, then he probably knew a great deal about our kind.

Without another glance at me or Violet, he strode out of the Cauldron, banging the door open as he left. Mateo brushed past him, frowning over his shoulder. I stepped over and leaned on the bar, arms crossed, watching my man come closer. His shoulder-length hair was pulled back away from his face, one wayward piece loose over an eye. He'd told me he'd be working on his latest commission in his studio most of the day. Those well-worn jeans, ripped at the knee, made my mouth water. I was sure he had one of those threadbare T-shirts on underneath his black hoodie. I wanted to pull off his hoodie and find out.

"I'm going with you to that guy's place," said Violet on my left behind me.

"The hell you are."

Scoffing like she was insulted, she said, "Why not?"

Leveling my are-you-kidding-me look at her, I rolled my eyes and turned back to Mateo, who'd caught sight of me, his tilted smile and roving gaze heating my skin and making my pulse flutter in my chest. I wondered how long it would take for the newness of our relationship to wear off, for my heart to not trip every time he stepped into the room. I hoped never.

"Well, you're not going alone." Violet pulled a rag from behind the bar and swiped it over the wooden counter. "That guy could get violent. He had that look about him."

"What guy?" asked Mateo, now in front of me, hands sliding around my waist, his mouth dipping to brush a sweet kiss over mine.

"That behemoth who just left," answered Violet. "Mateo, don't let her go alone."

His mouth worked mine open, his tongue taking a slick glide inside. One of his hands pressed at the small of my back, the other wrapped around my ponytail and tugged so he could have better access to my mouth. I clutched onto his hoodie, moaning as I sank against his six-and-a-half-foot frame. He was built leaner than Mr. Romano, but he was packed with sinuous muscle. And inside him lived a nearly nine-foot werewolf if I ever needed him. This was my safe place. My heaven on earth. My Christmas wish come true.

He broke our kiss. I chased his mouth, still hungry, but he gripped my ponytail tighter. "Why would you go to that guy's place?"

Fisting tighter on his hoodie for balance, I lifted onto my tiptoes and nipped his jaw. "I have to break his hex and meet his neighbor."

"I'll go with you," he offered, his voice dipping into a husky purr.

Flattening my feet, I glanced up to see a flash of gold roll over his eyes. Alpha wasn't happy about me going to some guy's place. I pressed a finger into the divot of his chin.

"Of course you're going with me."

He grinned back in reply, both of us just staring like the lovestruck dummies we were.

Violet rounded the bar to bus a two-top. "You do know we have customers, right?"

Not pulling my attention from Mateo, I slid my hands up his chest to lock around his neck. "One is flirting with JJ, and the other is buried in his newspaper."

"Still," she passed by us, carrying three beer mugs in each hand, "it's rude."

Sighing, I pulled out of Mateo's arms, glancing at my watch. "I'm off shift in thirty minutes, then just need to go take a quick shower."

He tugged on the bottom of my T-shirt, his index finger sliding over the skin of my belly. "New T-shirt?"

Looking down like I could forget my latest novelty shirt, I read the caption below Deadpool in a Santa suit: *Sit on my lap. I'll make your wish come true.*

"I'm getting in the Christmas spirit."

"I see that." He slid the back of his index finger along my skin above the edge of my jeans, sending a pleasant chill down my spine. Goosebumps tingled on my skin. When he looked up from where his hand glided under my shirt, his eyes flared more gold than brown. "When do I get you to myself, Evie?"

Shivering at the roughness in his voice, I replied a little breathlessly, "Soon. I have to get a shower and go break that hex first."

He leaned down and bit my earlobe, then licked away the sting. "I'm going crazy over here."

"Evie!" I jumped back out of Mateo's arms like a child caught with her hand in the cookie jar. I glanced down at the bulge in his jeans, kind of wishing I'd had my hand in *his* cookie jar.

"Yeah?" I circled to the sound of my sister Isadora hurrying into the bar.

Her blond waves streamed loosely around the shoulders of her pale green peasant blouse. She scurried around the tables, her flowy, cream-and-crimson skirt swishing, desperation in her bright green eyes. Isadora was my only sister with the same green eyes as my own.

"Hey, Mateo," she said in a rush before turning back to me, her arms full with a box of paper and ribbons pouring out the top. "Please tell me you can help me with these decorations. Clara asked me to make little paper books to go with the teacups on the tables. And everyone else has other party tasks to do."

"It's my party, too. What do I get?" Violet joined our circle, both hands on her hips, looking totally put out.

Isadora flipped her hair back out of her eyes, but it always slid forward again. "Livvy is taking care of yours, of course."

"Oh, okay. Good." Violet heaved a little sigh of relief and nodded her approval. "Livvy will make sure it's not *too* glittery." Then she continued on past the bar and into the kitchen.

Livvy had a darker edge and connected to Violet's black soul better than the rest of us. If anyone could figure out what would make her witchy self smile, it was Livvy.

Since Isadora and Livvy had returned from visiting our parents in Switzerland a week ago, they'd taken over all family business. On top of Isadora triple-checking the inventory at our metaphysical shop, Mystic Maybelle's, and Livvy interrogating Jules's new sous chef at the Cauldron, they'd dived into the party-planning for the twins—Clara and Violet.

Since the four of us had been holding down the fort while they were gone, and because I would rather be spending every second of free time with Mateo, I didn't mind at all.

Peeking into Isadora's box of small cover print-outs, tape, scissors, and so on, I replied, "I've got to go break a hex first, but then I'm all yours."

"Sweet! I knew I could count on you." She pecked a kiss on my cheek and swirled to leave again.

"What about me?" asked Mateo, taking hold of my hand with a squeeze, his brow raised in question.

I'd promised that tonight I'd finally stay at his place. Since my sisters had gotten back home, we'd had hardly any real time alone together. Except for one quickie, which was fantastic but, well, too quick. I sighed, ready to apologize.

"So sorry," said Isadora, winding back to us. "Here you go, pumpkin." She moved her box to a hip and pulled him down for a peck on the cheek. "Love having a hot, future brother-in-law."

"Hey!" I whined.

Isadora backed away and shrugged her shoulders with a cheeky grin. "Couldn't resist." With a wink, she spun and walked toward the back entrance, throwing over her shoulder, "That's the most action I've had in ages."

I shook my head at her. That's Isadora. Always finding ways to shock the shit out of people. She was a severe introvert but not actually shy at all around family and friends. Damn, I'd missed her.

Tugging Mateo toward the door, I sighed. "Come on. I've gotta go see that angry Italian and break his hex."

CHAPTER 2

~MATEO~

WE STOOD outside the black wrought iron gate surrounding the attractive duplex near Audubon Park. The fresh white paint with black trim and identical, glossy red-painted doors with gold knockers set this house off as one of the many renovated projects on this fashionable end of Magazine Street.

I opened the gate and pressed a hand to Evie's back, needing to touch her more than she needed me guiding her through.

"Which one?" I asked.

She glanced down at the business card in her hand

with Marcus Romano's handwritten address. A throaty growl rumbled in the back of my throat.

I don't like this asshole giving Evie his home address.

She asked for it, so settle down.

If he touches her, I'm breaking his fingers.

She has to touch him to break the hex. Chill out.

"That one." She pointed to the brick-paved walkway leading to the right.

Multicolored Christmas lights trimmed the other door on the left as well as the evergreen wreath. A family of three golden deer stood near the door on a small patch of lawn, their mechanical heads bobbing slowly as if to eat the grass. The baby fawn wore a red ribbon around its neck. There was a second scene on the lawn, two Christmas elves stacking presents, lit up in white lights. From the duplex on that side, Frank Sinatra's "Let It Snow" boomed from within. Though my werewolf hearing was more sensitive, it must've been easily heard by humans passing by on the sidewalk as well. The door and lawn on the right was bare, not one sign of holiday decorations.

Evie took in the Christmas decor on the opposite side as we walked up the short stoop. "I think I know why Mr. Romano had a hex put on him."

Before I could respond, the door swung open. On

instinct, I stepped in front of Evie and pushed her behind me. A rumbling growl vibrated in my chest.

Marcus Romano's deep frown morphed into surprise, most likely zeroing in on my eyes glowing gold. I knew when Alpha was exerting his presence, like now.

That's right, dickwad. Alpha is here. Better back the fuck up off my girl.

"Whoa, whoa, whoa!" Evie scrambled back around me. "Mr. Romano, this is my boyfriend, Mateo."

With one proprietary hand on her hip, I reached the other around her, offering to shake his hand.

Break his big, stupid nose.

Calm your ass down. We're here to support Evie.

The guy looked like he'd been through hell. His tie hung loosely from his collar, the top two buttons of his starched, white shirt undone. He held a tumbler of liquor in his right hand, and his nose was so swollen and red, he looked like he'd been stung by an entire hornet's nest.

"Sorry." He blinked and shook his head, shifting his drink into his left hand then shook mine. His rough palm was cold from holding the drink. "I was about to head next door."

"Why?" asked Evie.

His scowl returned. "Don't you hear that shit?"

"Frank Sinatra's Christmas album?"

"Yeah. That damn music!" He combed a hand to the back of his skull and turned, leaving the door open.

We followed inside, finding an immaculate living space. Stark with minimalist decor and paintings, sleek furniture in modernist style. Nothing out of place.

He knocked back what was in his glass. "Anyone want a drink?"

I shook my head at Evie, wanting to get out of here as soon as possible.

Evie surveyed the room. "No thanks."

Marcus stepped over to the granite island in his open kitchen where a bottle of bourbon sat. He poured a few fingers, then twisted back to us, exasperation written all over his face.

"It's that music." He took a gulp, then laughed maniacally. "No. It's everything. That witch is batshit crazy. And she's making *me* crazy. I can't even think straight." He drained his glass and slammed it down with a clatter on the granite.

"Come take a seat," said Evie, her voice lilting in that compassionate tone she'd used on me more than once when I'd been tortured by my own curse a few weeks ago.

He strode through the living room and sat on the sofa, rubbing his palms on his gray slacks. "Let's get this over with."

She walked behind the sofa and put her hands on his shoulders. "Just relax and close your eyes."

He exhaled heavily and did what she said. She closed her eyes, too, and squeezed his shoulder. With an inaudible whisper, she squeezed again. The electric sizzle of magic zapped in the air. Her fingers brightened with a glowing green sheen for two seconds then disappeared. The scent of magic—balmy energy and pungent earth—tingled my nose.

As for Marcus Romano's nose, it deflated back to its normal size with no redness or swelling whatsoever. Though it did look larger than it should be, but that seemed to be because it had been broken once or twice and had healed a little askew.

Evie patted his shoulder and said cheerily, "All done."

Marcus snapped his eyes open, catching my gaze first. But his hand immediately went to his nose, then he belted out a bark of laughter.

Evie had come around the sofa to stand next to me. "Mr. Romano, I need you to introduce me to your neighbor."

"Anything." He rose and turned toward the mantel above his fireplace, staring at his reflection and touching his nose, obviously making sure it was all back to normal. "You gonna give her a witch warning or something? A citation?"

Evie pressed her lips together before replying, "Not exactly. I'd like to resolve this conflict between you two."

He spun around, a pinch reappearing in the middle of his forehead. He scoffed. "I will never be friends with that witch."

"I don't need you to be friends. But if whatever problem is between you two isn't resolved, she can just put the hex back on you."

His full-on scowl returned. "Fuck that shit." He cut across toward the door. "Let's go."

We followed, walking down his stoop and around the walkway toward her holiday-decorated side. The Christmas music shut off before we stepped up to the small porch. Marcus clanked the knocker three times a bit too hard. Within seconds, the door swung open, revealing a pretty Black woman, her curly hair bouncing on her shoulder, held back with a red bandana headband. She wore no makeup except lip-gloss. With naturally thick, black lashes that curled around hazel eyes she didn't need mascara. She was stunning. As she swung the door wider, a wave of apples and spice wafted out the door.

Her gaze narrowed on Marcus first, her hand propped on her hip where a sliver of tawny skin was exposed between her jeans and short-cropped red sweater decorated with sparkly silver snowflakes.

"Tia?" Evie's surprised tone drew my attention back to her.

"Evie! Oh, my God." The neighbor reached forward and jerked Evie into a tight hug. "It's so good to see you."

Evie huffed out a laugh. "It's been a while."

"Not since Aunt Beryl's last sage party."

Tia was tall and curvy, similar in build to Evie. She pulled back and opened the door wider, stepping out of the way. "Come on in."

Marcus glanced back at me, dumbfounded. I shrugged. We followed the ladies inside.

"So I guess you're responsible for Marcus's new nose job." Tia smirked over her shoulder, her gaze flicking over Marcus, a spark of heat and appreciation lighting her face before she looked away.

She wants him.

You know what? You might be right.

I know I'm right. One thing I know is when a woman wants a man. I'm an expert.

"Guilty," said Evie.

Marcus crossed his arms, staring around the place and grimacing like he'd smelled something offensive. The living room was draped in greenery, white lights, snow globes, and a collection of glittery snowmen figurines on her mantel. In between a myriad of holiday displays were apple-cinnamon and pine-scented candles.

"So you're friends with this witch," Marcus said to Evie, harsh and accusing.

"I am." Her gaze moved to mine. "Tia's aunt is my mother's best friend. We sort of grew up together."

"Sort of?" Tia's bright smile made Marcus's frown deepen. "We took weekly spell lessons together from my aunt and her mom for about five years."

"But I hired you." Marcus stood straighter. "If you plan to take her side just because you're friends—"

"That's not how I roll, Mr. Romano, so just calm your britches."

Tia's smile spread wider as she stared at Marcus. "Yeah, *Mr.* Romano. Calm your britches."

"Tia—" he growled, but in a different way than he'd been huffing at us since we'd arrived.

That's a have-sex-with-me growl. Know it well.

Tia was oblivious to his aggressive mannerisms. "I can put another spell on you, you know?"

"That's why I'm here," said Evie, injecting more professionalism in her tone and clearing her throat. "So tell us why you did it in the first place."

Marcus uncrossed his arms and took a step toward Tia, jabbing a finger in the air at her. "It's because I can't stand your fucking Christmas music, isn't it?"

Tia's brows rose. "Watch your language, *Marcus*." A

hand went back to her hip, making her sweater rise, exposing more of her belly and a diamond-stud piercing on her navel. Marcus zoned in on it.

Can you blame the guy? I know what would take that frown off his face. And put a bigger smile on hers.

"Tia." Evie pleaded softly. "Tell us what this is about. You can't just hex people because they hate Christmas."

"I don't hate Christmas," snarled Marcus. "Just all the silly shit that goes with it."

Tia rolled her eyes. "I can handle his constant bitching. That doesn't bother me. But when he killed my snowman, that was it."

Marcus snorted like a bull. "I *told* you. It was an accident."

"Ha! You must think me a fool. His head was completely decapitated."

"I swear, Tia. I didn't do it on purpose. If you'd just listen to me—"

"I did listen to you. And if you think I'm believing that stupid excuse you tried to tell me, you're crazy."

By this point, they were both in each other's faces. Marcus looked like his head was about to explode.

Again. I know what would end this feud. It starts with an "S" and ends with an "X."

"Okay, okay!" Evie physically put herself between them and pushed them apart. "Tia, Marcus says it's an accident, but you don't believe him. What if he buys you a new one?"

"I offered to do that already," growled Marcus.

"I don't need your money." Tia crossed her arms under her breasts. "I want an apology."

"I'm fucking sorry! Is that good enough?"

"Ha! No. It is not."

Marcus turned to me and gestured with both hands at Tia. "See! She's crazy. I can't reason with this."

Tell him my idea.

Shut it.

"This is what's going to happen," said Evie, turning and facing both of them like a mother to her unruly children.

In that moment, I could see her facing off our own wild litter of kids one day, giving them that maternal glare and no-nonsense speech.

***Our* wild litter.**

The very idea made me want to snatch her close and haul ass back to my place and start making babies. It also made my heart expand another inch, swelling at the mere idea of a world where little Evies and Mateos ran around raising all kinds of hell in our household. Our household. I wanted that more than anything.

"Marcus, you're going to buy her a new snowman for the yard, the exact same kind she had before and set it up for her. Tia, you're going to accept it with grace and keep your Christmas music to normal decibels. What I heard when I walked up was an obvious attempt to annoy your neighbor. Will that appease both parties?"

"Fine by me," grumbled Marcus, his gaze fixed on Tia.

"I need an act of atonement," said Tia, her pert nose in the air away from Marcus.

"Of course you do," he sneered. "What the hell does that mean anyway?"

Ignoring him, Tia pointed at Marcus with serious accusation in her voice, "He was so mean to me, Evie. I need atonement."

"What does that mean?" I asked.

Evie swiveled back to me. "It's common for witches in dispute. The offending member needs to do an action that proves they're sorry. A verbal apology isn't quite enough. We follow the whole *actions speak louder than words* creed."

"What the hell do you want?" asked Marcus with a sneer. "I'm not groveling on my knees or anything to her," he bit out to Evie.

I bet he would if she asked nicely. While naked.

Evie clasped her hands together in front of her. "I have the perfect idea." She glanced between the two, landing back on Marcus. "You're both coming to a party tomorrow night at our pub, the Cauldron at nine o'clock. It's a Karaoke party." She gave her best I-mean-it glare to Marcus. "You'll sing a Christmas song of my choice without protest. That's the deal."

"Yesssss!" Tia jumped up and down, giddily clapping her hands.

Evie swung her attention to Tia. "You're singing it with him."

"Me? But he's the one who—"

"Nope. Tia, I know you've been overtly annoying with the music and who knows what else. This will be an act you'll do together, and finally put behind you all this animosity toward each other. Let bygones be bygones."

Marcus rolled his eyes, which actually made me chuckle. "This some kind of a Christmas party?"

"My twin sisters' birthday party actually."

Tia beamed another smile, her eyes sparkling. "Clara and Vi's? Awesome! I can't wait."

"Of course you can't," he shook his head pityingly at Tia. "Are we done here?"

She just bounced past him with a superior tilt of her chin and opened the door for us.

Evie grabbed my hand as she passed, following Marcus.

"See you tomorrow night," said Tia excitedly.

We said our goodbyes and left through the wrought iron gate toward my vintage Chevy truck parked on the street. My hands itched to hold her, to bury my face into her neck, to feel her skin against mine. This craving I had for her was constant, clawing, desperate. Somehow, I knew that craving would never ease up. At least I could control my urges now. I could keep my hands to myself—mostly. Better than before anyway, when Alpha had me so on edge. When I was under that witch's spell.

In public, I could mask my burning need, subdue the beast with a simple look from her, a brief touch. But in private, I took advantage of every single second. Like now. When we walked up to my truck, I dragged her into my arms, pressing her against the passenger door. She gasped. I covered her mouth with mine and breathed her in.

She was so perfect. Her body. Her mind. Her heart. She turned me on in every possible way, and I couldn't keep my hands from roaming.

"Evie," I growled against her lips. "Sweet Evie."

She whimpered and slipped her tongue into my mouth. Gripping her hips, I pressed my pelvis to hers, grinding my hard dick in that perfect hollow between her legs. A shaky moan escaped her mouth as I pulled back and scraped my teeth across her bottom lip. Pressing my forehead to hers, I held her half-lidded gaze.

"I need you tonight."

We need her every night.

She gave me a little whimpered cry of protest. "But Isadora."

"Shit." I closed my eyes. "I forgot."

She threaded her fingers into my hair, ghosting across my neck. "I could stand her up for a little while."

That's right. Fuck them. Our needs are more important.

She slid her hand below the collar of my hoodie, grazing her nails along my nape. Hard. I groaned, my dick swelling at her touch.

"No," I forced myself to sigh. "I don't want to be the boyfriend who pulls you away from your sisters."

"Why are you such a good guy?"

I am *not* a good guy, baby.

She's fully aware that you're not good. She's talking to me.

I kissed her hard, then pulled away and opened the passenger door. As she got in, I put a finger under her chin and tilted her face up to me.

"But tomorrow night—" holding her gaze, her deep green eyes rounded at something she saw in mine —"you're all mine."

She smiled, a blush noticeable even in the dark. "Yes, sir."

Got that damn right.

CHAPTER 3

~EVIE~

ISADORA and I had finished making the little paper imitations of Clara's favorite historical romance novels around midnight, then were up early to clean and decorate the Cauldron. That had taken till late afternoon to get it to Isadora's satisfaction. Now, we were finally setting the tables, which was allegedly last on her list before we showered and dressed for the party.

I propped the replicas of Julia Quinn's *Just Like Heaven* and Kerrigan Byrne's *The Highlander* alongside the miniature tea set. A raised silver plate of votive candles centered each table. Not yet lit. Livvy followed behind us, ornamenting the centerpiece with her feature for Violet. I circled back to the last table to get a good look.

"Whoa. Livvy, that's freaking gorgeous."

"Isn't it?"

Isadora flipped her wild hair over one shoulder so she could lean in close and focus on balancing the replica of Lisa Kleypas's *Seduce Me at Sunrise* just right. "So humble, Livvy."

She leveled one of her superior looks at Isadora before shrugging. "I see no point in being coy. It looks fabulous."

She'd recreated the blooming orchid tattoo that dominated most of Violet's right shoulder. Violet's ink was done in intense shading of black and blue, but Livvy had created a silk version with deep indigo and purplish hues at the center. In the midst of that was a sprinkle of glitter that shimmered silver and seemed to move like raindrops sliding along the petals as you circled around the table.

I tilted my head and raised an accusatory brow. "You used magic."

She shrugged innocently again before twisting her jet-black waves up onto her head, tying it into a messy bun.

"No one said I couldn't. It's just a little glamour spell. It can't hurt anyone."

"Until Jules catches on. You know how she is about using magic for frivolous things."

Livvy leaned over a table and set another of her blooming silk creations next to a miniature copy of Eloisa James's *When Beauty Tamed the Beast*. "Beauty is not frivolous," she murmured.

Smiling at her response, I continued onto my next table. Livvy was a lover of beauty. But not just the physical kind. Though of us sisters, she was the most arresting with her black hair, pale skin, and piercing blue eyes that could shift from pale blue-green to deep midnight, depending on her mood. There was also something about the shape of Livvy's features. They were similar to the rest of ours, but more severe, exaggerated. Her eyes rounder, cheekbones sharper, and her lips overfull. Add that to her distinctive fashion sense, she stuck out in that uniquely beautiful way that turned heads.

Like now. While I was in my everyday attire of jeans and a T-shirt, Isadora wore a loose-fitting, beige Boho shirt with hunter-green leggings and cardigan sweater. But Livvy wore a long-sleeved black lace top that hugged her tiny waist, also accented by a red velvet belt, then flared with loose chiffon around her curvy hips. That did nothing to hide her fantastic legs draped in tight, white leggings embellished with a subtle design of ivy crawling up her legs. If any of us looked like a witch, it was Livvy.

I'd like to say she played up the persona as a walking billboard for Mystic Maybelle's, but the truth was that her style matched her personality. Eccentric, bold, and sexy.

"Oh, my goodness!" Clara stopped in her tracks from the kitchen with a tray in her hand. Her face lit up, sparkling as much as the tiara on her head. "It looks so beautiful!" she practically squealed.

Already dressed for the party in a shimmery blueish silver mini-dress, in addition to her crown, she wore her red birthday sash with silver writing, *Princess For A Day*.

"Y'all are the best sisters ever!" She set the tray down on the buffet table beside the silver-domed servers.

Isadora skipped over to her and wrapped her in a hug, then gave her a smacking kiss on the cheek. "Anything for our baby sister."

Clara hugged her back, cheek to cheek, saying sweetly, "I'm not the baby. Violet is."

"Close enough."

"Clara, you look like *Elsa* from Frozen."

"Thank you, Livvy!" She gasped with joy. "You know what? I could dig up 'Let It Go' for the Karaoke playlist."

Isadora and I shared a look. It was Clara's party so

we'd let her sing to her tone-deaf heart's content. But it didn't make it any easier to know we were in for a doozy of a night with the Karaoke machine. At least, Clara was all about sharing, which meant she wouldn't hog the stage.

I joined Clara, linking an arm with her to face our handiwork. "It really does look pretty, doesn't it?"

White Christmas lights draped the room. Starting at the center of the beamed ceiling, we'd fanned outward, creating a starburst pattern that warmed the bar with a magical glow. The tables were lovely and would add to the cozy ambiance when the votive candles were lit. Greenery draped the walls with red ribbon and gold beads twining together. Each wall featured an oversized wreath with gold and silver balls and lit brightly with white lights. Our Christmas tree in the corner next to the stage where the Karaoke was set up brightened the room even more.

Just then, a man tried to open the door and found it locked.

I gasped. "The sign!" I grabbed it off the bar where I'd left it and jogged over to the door, holding it up for the man on the other side of the window to read. "Sorry!"

He read the sign: *Closed for private party*. Then gave me the thumbs up before ambling on. I taped the sign in the window, facing out.

"What's on the menu?" asked Livvy, stepping over to the tray Clara had brought in.

"This is a sampler for the party. Jules knew you'd be hungry after setting up all day."

"Bacon. Yummm." I grabbed a bacon-wrapped shrimp and asparagus tip, greedily gobbling it down. "Freaking awesome."

"She did those prosciutto-wrapped dates you love so much too, Livvy."

Isadora picked up her clipboard, checking off her party to-do list. The rest of us descended on our appetizer-style dinner when three solid knocks sounded against the windowpane. Mateo stood on the other side, looking absolutely amazing. I froze with a mini eggroll halfway to my mouth. Holding my gaze through the glass, his small smile creased wider into a devilish one.

"Damn, Evie," said Isadora with a hip-bump next to me, her Sharpie fine-point poised over her clipboard. "That man is fine with a capital F."

"Is he ever," I mumbled, wiping my greasy fingers on a napkin as I rushed over to unlock the door.

Dressed in a black Henley, dark jeans, and a seductive smile, his wavy hair loose, his broody eyes hinted at devilry. It was like a French cologne ad had sex with a rock video. And their baby was standing at my door, giving me a you're-going-to-go-up-in-flames-in-my-bed-tonight look.

"Hi," I said breathlessly, grinning like a fiend when I let him in.

"Hi." He mirrored the same tone with suggestive meaning before swooping down with a brief but hard kiss, only a tease of tongue. Holding me by the hips against him, he licked his lips. "Mmm. Bacon."

"That's what I said."

By the time we'd extricated ourselves from each other's arms and turned around, we were alone, except for Isadora who was intently focused on her clipboard.

Clara poked her head back in from the swinging kitchen door. "Isadora," she yell-whispered, like we couldn't hear or see her.

Isadora popped her head up and looked shocked, like she'd just noticed us. "Oh. Sorry." She grinned sheepishly, heading for the kitchen.

I huffed out a laugh, lacing my fingers behind his neck. "I think they're starting to feel guilty that they're keeping us apart so much with the party."

"Good." He leaned down and kissed a trail down the side of my neck. "Because when I can finally tear you away, I'm holding you hostage for a while."

I luxuriated in the sensation of his perfect lips sweeping over my pulse. "Fine by me."

"Evie!" called Jules. I swiveled my head. She stood in the doorway of the kitchen. "Oops. Sorry."

I heaved out a sigh and backed out of Mateo's arms. "What's up?"

She pointed a whisk at me, as she'd obviously remembered something mid-whisk in the kitchen. "The cake. Can you go pick it up?"

"But I still need to shower." I glanced at the clock on the wall. Friends were arriving at seven-ish for dinner, then Karaoke was kicking off right after.

"I'll get the cake," said Mateo.

"You will?"

He hauled me back into his arms, fingers spread wide on my waist, then he bent his head close to my ear. "Go get cleaned up. But I'll still be getting you dirty again later tonight."

I pulled out of his arms, walking backwards. "Promises, promises." With a wink, I turned and headed toward the back entrance, the quickest way to our house through the alley. As much as I loved my sisters, I couldn't wait for this party to be over.

CHAPTER 4

~MATEO~

Hands in my pockets, I ambled across the street toward the bakery. Among the trendy and chic shops sprawled down Magazine Street, Queen of Tarts stood out in vibrant Technicolor. The window display was piled with tiers of strawberry macarons, chocolate eclairs, lemon and raspberry tarts, mini blueberry cobbler pies, and all sizes and colors of cakes with swooping decorative icing.

A whiff of cigarette smoke cut into my drooling along with a sudden push of my primal hungers. Alpha growled deep in my chest in response. He enjoyed the pull of darker cravings that a grim reaper could produce. On the corner of the bakery, his back propped against the wall was the grim I'd talked to on occasion. The same one who gave me the information I needed about Evie the night I'd met her.

Aloof but watchful, he leaned his tall frame against the brick wall, one hand in his leather jacket pocket, the other at his side with a cigarette dangling from his fingers. He didn't acknowledge he'd noticed me, but I knew he had. Grims were known for their observational skills and their ability to remain basically invisible, adding to their air of mystery among our kind.

"Hey." I called out with a lift of my chin as I walked over.

His dark gaze slid my way before he lifted his cigarette and took a deep drag in response. Super friendly, this one.

Did he just sneer at us?

No. That's a normal look for him.

I'll wipe it off his face with my fist if he isn't careful.

Calm down. He's a friend.

And while I knew for a fact I could beat this guy in a physical fight if I needed to, which I didn't, I always worried what kinds of powers grims kept hidden. I'd heard about a vampire who'd attacked a grim in a bar in the French Quarter last year. Within two seconds of the vampire putting his hands on the grim, he fell back onto the ground, curled into a fetal position, screaming and begging for it to stop. The vampire fell into a comatose state and needed a witch to bring him out of it. A month later. The vampire didn't remember anything, couldn't tell anyone what the "it" was that he wanted to stop. Only that he had a bone-deep fear of grims afterwards.

So yeah, I wasn't going to fight him because Alpha thought he was sneering at us. As I sidled up to him, his sharp features, gaze never shifting from the street gave me the impression of a jaguar in the brush, watching and waiting for prey to suddenly fall into his line of sight. I was about to ask him exactly what he was looking for when he shocked me by speaking first.

"Things worked out well with the witch, Eveleen, didn't they?" His gaze finally cut to me, a subtle smirk ticking up one side of his wide mouth.

Fucking right things worked out. Better stop smiling like that when you say her name, grim.

I nodded, both hands in my pockets, agreeing much more civilly than the wolf in my head. "They did."

He measured me longer than felt comfortable, longer than he had before. Alpha bristled inside me. An edgy anxiety rushed underneath my skin, pushing me with aggression. That might just be from standing too close to a grim this long. When I thought he might say something more about Evie, he just gave me a tight nod.

"Cool."

I pointed over my shoulder. "Just picking up a cake for her sisters' birthday party."

Why I told him that, I have no idea. And why a suddenly intense expression tightened his angular features into utter stillness, I also had no idea. There was a glimpse of something in his gaze, there and gone so fast, I wondered if I'd seen it.

For some damn reason, it had me opening my mouth again, knowing full well I might be overstepping, even as the beloved boyfriend of Evie. I hesitated, but that intangible knowing of what it was like to be lonely—because I'd known that feeling better than anyone, until Evie—had me asking anyway.

"If you want to come, they've got plenty of drinks and food."

For a split second, he gave me the most shocked expression I'd ever seen on his always-calm-and-cool face. When he shifted his mask of indifference back into place, he dropped his cigarette and crushed it with his boot.

"You're inviting me to Clara's birthday party?"

The way he said her name—so familiar—unsettled me a little. I didn't think they knew each other that well. I cleared my throat. "Clara and Violet's, yeah." I shrugged a shoulder. "If you want."

He stared at me, saying nothing, the wheels turning in his head. This exchange had suddenly become so strange and I was wondering what the hell had propelled me to ask him. The awkward silence stretched, his dark eyes measuring me again.

"Anyway," I thumbed over my shoulder, "I've gotta get the cake."

Without another glance, I pushed through the door of Queen of Tarts, jingling the bell overhead and immediately salivating at the overwhelming smells of sweets and pastries. A few seconds later, a robust woman with a cheery face and snow-white hair appeared from the swinging door leading to the back. She wore an apron that read: *All you knead is love.*

"Well, good afternoon, handsome." She wiped some purple icing on her apron. "What can I get for you?"

"I'm here to pick up the cake for the Savoie's."

Her face brightened even more, her round cheeks already rosy pink. "Clara and her sister's cake?" She turned to the counter behind the register where a large white cake box sat. "I hope she likes it."

She set it on the counter and opened the lid. For a second, I just stared, trying to soak in the fact that this was actually made of milk, eggs, flour, and sugar.

"Wow."

"You think she'll like it?"

"Which one?" I kept staring.

"Clara. She's a regular customer and such a sweet young lady, I wanted to do something she'd love."

The cake was a large rectangular fantasyland. Overlaying the white icing was a green forest with a prancing unicorn, a garden of blue roses, a fairy with pink wings, a mermaid's green tail flipping out of a lagoon, and a purple dragon breathing fire into the air. In the midst of the wonderland was a perfectly scripted happy birthday message to the twins.

The owner, for she seemed to be the owner, shuffled behind the counter. "I hope that she'll like it. When her older sister ordered the cake, she just said to do something whimsical."

"She'll love it," I assured her with complete honesty.

"And her sister? I've never met her but figured they probably like some of the same things. Twins and all."

Huffing out a short laugh, I quickly recovered with a sharp nod. "I'm sure she'll love it, too."

Violet would hate this cake. She might like the dragon.

If it were roasting a man on fire, she would. Man-eater, that one.

She taped the box shut and told me it had been paid for already, so I was on my way. The grim, whose name I still didn't know, was nowhere to be seen. Funny, he probably knew my name, date of birth, and social security number, but I knew next to nothing about him. Besides the fact he was a chain-smoker and worked for Ruben Dubois on occasion.

Using the alleyway between the Cauldron and Mystic Maybelle's, I headed back through the kitchen entrance. Jules was leaning against a counter, tilting back a glass of merlot. The cooktops were all wiped down and clean, her prepping for dinner finally done.

"Got the cake," I gestured if it wasn't obvious enough.

"Thank you, Mateo." She set aside the now empty glass, then took the cake from me and headed into the bar.

Though I was more accustomed to seeing Jules with a permanent scowl on her face, there was a strong agitated energy around her that made me wonder if she actually had a reason to be so prickly tonight.

Following her out into the cozy ambience of the bar, a stark contrast from the fluorescent lights of the kitchen, I asked, "Everything good?"

JJ was behind the bar pouring a jug of white liquid into a giant, glass punch bowl.

"Everything's just fine and dandy." Her sarcastic sing-song voice told me otherwise.

"You sure about that?"

She grumbled something as she opened the cake

box and set it on one end of the buffet table. She didn't even blink at the masterpiece of confection fantasy. Just turned herself about and marched back into the kitchen with a loud slap against the swinging door.

I arched a brow at JJ, the bartender who'd worked for the sisters for years and who'd also become like a brother to them. He was one of the few humans who knew what they truly were, and who knew what I was, for that matter. Most humans had no clue there were supernaturals walking among them, and we preferred it that way. But JJ was in on the family secret, very protective of the sisters.

He stared at the swinging kitchen door where she'd disappeared, then shook his head as he opened another jug of some kind of white concoction.

"I have no idea." He pulled a silver ice bucket from a bottom cabinet. "But I'd stay away from her tonight if I were you."

"Not a problem." Though cordial, Jules and I still weren't exactly friendly.

"Here." He scooped some ice into a tumbler than dipped the punch ladle into the bowl. "Try this."

"What is it?" I reached for the glass. "White Russian?"

He grinned, his white teeth bright against his dark beard. He crossed his arms over a muscular chest, his biceps stretching his maroon T-shirt. "My special eggnog."

"Oh, hell," came a man's voice to our right. "No damn way, Jeremy. That shit should be illegal."

JJ rolled his eyes at his best friend Charlie who strolled in from the back entrance dressed to the nines in gray corduroy pants, a starched white shirt and a festive red vest with silver bells stitched in shiny satin. I'd originally thought Charlie was JJ's boyfriend, but Evie swears they're just friends. Still, there's something there.

Definitely something there.

"Don't drink it," warned Charlie, pulling up a stool next to mine.

JJ shrugged, still grinning. I took a swig. Cinnamon, spices. Bourbon. Not bad. Too sweet for my taste—*holy fuck,* what was that? Burning flames licked down my throat, singeing my nostrils on the way down.

"Whoa." My voice was rusty from one scorching sip. "That's potent."

It'll put some lead in your pencil, for damn sure. Not that we need help with that.

Charlie crossed his legs and propped an elbow on the bar-top, his hands clasped. "The danger is when you finish your first drink. You stop feeling the burn. Then you're in a world of trouble."

I set the glass back on the bar with an apologetic

smile for JJ. "Sorry, man. Gotta keep my wits about me tonight."

"Any special reason?"

Then a whiff of something utterly delicious wafted into the room. It set my body on full alert, rolling over my skin with a tantalizing brush. Jasmine shampoo, cocoa butter lotion, and clean woman.

Evie.

Angling toward the back hallway, I watched her walk toward me with the devil in her eyes, wearing a denim mini-skirt with a black sweater, accentuating her pretty figure, her hair down in auburn waves around her shoulders. I shook my head, and she grinned wider, knowing exactly what she was doing to me.

We leave this party in one hour.

Two tops.

One.

I wasn't going to argue with him. One sounded fucking fantastic to me.

CHAPTER 5

~EVIE~

THE BUFFET DINNER of gourmet appetizers was delicious, the cake amazing, and the drinks ever-flowing. The party had adjourned to the stage in the corner of the pub where Livvy managed the Karaoke music, getting things loud and rowdy. Everyone laughed, sang, heckled the singers, and seemed to be having a fabulous time.

Except my werewolf. His hooded gaze hadn't left me for one second all night. Except for a brief few minutes he talked to his cousin, Nico, who dropped by the party. And yeah, I'd noticed Nico's rapt attention on my sister Violet. The second birthday girl actually still wore her tiara, which Clara made with bright stones "to match her hair," she said. And her sash, *Queen For A Day*, was a little tattered from the night's events.

"Why does she get 'queen' and you get 'princess'?" Mateo asked.

He leaned across my lap so Clara could hear him over Isadora and Belinda, one of our servers and longtime friends, singing rather badly Beyonce's "Single Ladies." Mateo's palm wrapped around my bare knee, giving me an erotic tingle and a promise of what's to come. I wiggled, but he clamped his fingers harder, daring me to shake him off with a flicker of gold in his eyes. I pretended complete and total interest in what Clara was saying when Mateo damn well knew his possessive touches were making me crazy.

But who could I blame? I'd worn this outfit on purpose, to drive him a little crazy. It was all on me. Now, if he knew what I wore underneath this skirt—nothing—he'd have tossed me caveman-style over his shoulder and taken me back to his place. The only reason we were still here and not ripping each other's clothes off and tumbling naked around his apartment was because I was still waiting on Tia and Marcus to show up.

"That's easy," said Clara, forking up a bite of her third piece of cake. "Queens are assertive, demanding, and rather unbending. That's pretty much Violet."

"True." Throwing an arm around Clara's shoulder, I asked, "And what about princesses?"

"We're supportive, cheery, and only sometimes rebellious."

Mateo leaned into me, sliding his hand along the opposite thigh and up to grip the knee farthest from him. "And are you sometimes rebellious, Clara?"

She scraped the last dollop of purple icing into her mouth, gave us innocent doe eyes, shrugged and popped up to carry her empty plate to the back. Mateo's eyes followed her for a second then he leaned in to whisper, "I think your sweet and innocent sister has some secrets."

I watched her go, wondering if that were even possible. Jules had been texting furiously in the back since the party began, but now she was knocking back eggnog after eggnog. JJ was eyeing her with concern, and now so was I. What bug had gotten up her butt?

Then my eyes caught on a surprising someone leaning against one of the wooden columns in the middle of the pub, watching the stage. Well, maybe watching. I couldn't see where his eyes were aimed from here. They were dark and hooded in the shadow of his black hair that hung across his forehead.

"How'd he get in?"

Mateo glanced behind us. "Huh."

"You don't seem surprised that a grim is crashing our party."

"I invited him earlier. Saw him when I picked up the cake."

"Your friends with him?" My eyes widened, my voice rising with excitement. "How come I didn't know this!"

"Not exactly friends." He pulled my legs up and over until they were crossing his lap.

"But you invited him here?" It's not that I didn't like the guy, I just didn't know him. He was kind of a fixture on Magazine Street, but no one seemed to even know his name.

Mateo shrugged one shoulder. "He's helped me out before."

"What's his name?"

He laughed. "No idea."

I was going to interrogate him further, but then Tia and Marcus waltzed in from the back entrance where I'd told them to enter.

"Yes! They're here."

Popping up, I waved them over. To my utter delight and embarrassment, Mateo's fingers slid along the skin of the back of my thigh, edging along the hem of my mini-skirt. Tossing him a heated look over my shoulder, his gaze was transfixed on his own fingers.

When he looked up, I decided to kick this up to the next level and tell him I was going commando.

"What?"

I opened my mouth, but then Livvy stood in front of the microphone to the hoots and hollers of our friends, then said, "Thank you, everyone, for joining us tonight to celebrate the birthdays of my beloved sisters." Another round of cheers. "Now is the time Clara and Violet come up on stage and sing their birthday duet song, which I've picked out myself."

That's when Livvy smiled, bending her slender bare leg in her red velvet corset dress and angled her shoulder down, making her look like a femme fatale of the worst kind. Loud cat calls hooted from Finny, our dishwasher, and his buddies he'd brought tonight.

"Come on up, ladies," said Livvy in her husky voice, giving Finny a playful wink. Poor guy wouldn't know what to do if she was actually serious. She was too much for him.

Clara literally dragged a belligerent Violet up to the stage. Violet was still rolling her eyes when the first few notes of "Perfect" by Ed Sheeran echoed in the bar. Of course, Livvy picked an Ed Sheeran song, Clara's favorite artist. Clara started off the first verse, the audience clapping and offering encouragement. I was thankful our friends were tolerant, because she sounded just awful. No other way to say it.

"That's what I'll sound like," muttered Marcus, sidling up next to me.

"Probably," agreed Tia.

He exhaled a loud breath. "Whatever. Let's get this over with."

I pointed at the stage. "Go on up and tell Livvy you're here. She knows you're coming and is ready for you."

As they sauntered off, Mateo wrapped an arm around my waist and pulled me back onto his lap. He angled me sideways, banding an arm around my hip and spreading one hot, callused hand on my thigh. It was hard to think with his hands on me.

He nuzzled my hair aside, brushing his lips across my neck, then whispered, "Almost ready to go?"

"Mmhmm," was all I could manage.

Then my sister Violet started to sing, and a hush fell over the bar. She sang the verse about dancing in the dark, her melodious voice hitting every note with clarity and heated emotion. It was beautiful and intense and it pissed me off how utterly amazing Violet's voice was, yet she always refused to sing. She said it wasn't a gift she could use to do something good in the world. But holy hell, to hear her voice, it was hypnotic, haunting. It was like magic traveling in soundwaves, trembling on the air, and singing to my soul. Even Mateo had stilled his hands, though he pulled me close against him.

"Damn," he muttered.

"I know," I whispered back.

I glanced at Nico, who sat forward, staring, his elbows on his knees, hands casually clasped. It would've been convincing if it weren't for his knuckles going white with the tension of squeezing his fingers together so tight. Interesting.

The song came to a close, but before Tia and Marcus could even stand and approach Livvy, Jules stumbled up the two steps and grabbed the microphone from Clara. She muffled it in her hand and said something back to Livvy who gave her a careful once-over, then flipped back to her laptop with the digital music she'd hooked up to the speakers and Karoake machine.

"What is going on?" asked Mateo.

Completely transfixed, I couldn't answer. You have to understand. Jules was always in control. Always. No exceptions. Calm. Cool. And I had never seen her drunk. Ever. She allowed herself a glass of merlot at the end of the day. Maybe two. But that's it. What I was seeing right now was an anomaly, like Deadpool walking onscreen in *Lord of the Rings*. It just shouldn't be happening. But it totally was. The swaying mess up on stage was the sad result of JJ's lethal eggnog and whatever fury had worked her into drinking that much in the first place.

Jules cleared her throat. "Gotta song I wanna ded-cate."

Nico turned around from the row in front of us. "Did she say something about a dead cat?"

"Lis'n up!"

Finny and his crew laughed. Then he yelled encouragingly, "Whatcha got for us, Jules?"

She held a finger up for us to hold on a minute. Pinning the mic between her jean-clad legs, she unbuttoned and whipped off her chef's coat that she hadn't bothered to take off yet. When she tossed it offstage like it was a rag, I knew she was completely wasted. No way would she do that if she was anywhere close to sober.

Then she smoothed down her white T-shirt, pulled the mic from between her legs and propped a hand on her hip, standing ramrod straight. She was the most petite of all of us, so that small gesture did nothing to make her look bigger. Jules could usually make a six-foot-tall man wither with one glowering stare of her steel-gray eyes. Right now, she could barely focus, so her mean-girl pose was having zero effect.

She pointed to Finny, her finger then zipping from one man in the audience to another. "This goes out to *alllll* the assholes of the world!"

A collective hoot of laughter and cheers erupted when the music started, and though my oldest sister, the most powerful witch in New Orleans, was drunk off her ass, she started singing the hell out of Alanis Morisette's "You Oughta Know." With her fist in the air, her short, straight hair swinging in her eyes, and her voice claiming how it just wasn't fair and the cross she had to bear and he just oughta know, I burst into laughter. She had everyone rising out of their seats, clapping and singing along with her, escalating Jules's madness to a new level.

Not just madness. Magic. I could feel it eking off of her, and that had the laughter dying in my throat, replaced immediately by fear. Isadora glanced at me two seconds before she sprinted up onto the stage and grabbed Jules around the waist, ripping the mic from her hand. Jules was using magic and she hadn't even known it. With her level of power, she could've punched a hole in the room and accidentally knocked some people out, or worse. This is why Jules had to keep herself under control.

"That's enough," Isadora was mumbling, grappling with Jules who grabbed the mic again.

"Thank you, everybody! Come again next week!" She cackled. Yes, cackled, like an actual witch.

But our crowd of friends laughed and cheered more. Isadora wrestled her down the steps and toward the back hallway. Before I could go help, JJ was there, probably asking what I was thinking. Isadora shook her head and walked off with Jules alone.

"Why don't we switch gears and change to something totally different?" Livvy called from the stage before handing the mic over to Tia.

Marcus stood at the second mic, looking so out of place and completely miserable, as sleighbells started jingling.

Tia began singing "Let It Snow." Marcus found me in the audience and glowered. I arched a brow at him, then he joined in. The great thing about our friends is that they were just as easily entertained by the change in tunes, merrily singing along. Clara jumped up onstage, wrapping an arm around Tia and giving her a side-hug. By the end of the song, Tia was beaming, Marcus was smirking and looked almost happy, and the place was full of Christmas cheer. That's when Mateo stood and swooped me up into his arms in a bridal carry.

I yelped. "What are you doing?"

"Taking you home."

"Home?"

His heated look was all I got in response. Then he headed out the back door and down Magazine Street and took me home.

CHAPTER 6

~EVIE~

HOW COULD I possibly be nervous after all the times we'd had sex since we'd gone from friends to lovers? I don't know, but I was. Maybe nervous wasn't exactly the right word. If you could mash-up anticipation, hunger, and desperation into one feeling, that would be it.

He set me on my feet at the bottom of the stairs of his apartment that sat above his workshop and studio. Rushing up the stairs before him, I remembered the first time we'd had sex. That in itself had my blood pumping harder. Once I made the landing, I walked over to the living room and shrugged out of my jacket.

I don't know why, but I had a wild streak tonight. Maybe it was that one glass of JJ's eggnog. Maybe it was Jules's wild performance. But something made me want to poke the bear. The wolf, actually. When I turned, my breath caught in my throat, because my wolf was staring right back at me. Mateo's eyes had gone fiery gold. Alpha was in the room with us.

I stepped backward around the coffee table and picked up the remote. "You want to watch a movie?"

He shucked off his boots with a steady shaking of his head, his hot gaze never leaving me.

I set down the remote and toed off my flats. "How about a game of Scrabble or something?"

He didn't bother to respond that time, just reached back with both hands and pulled his shirt over his shoulders and his head, tossing it aside.

Now I couldn't breathe at all. Not when punched in the face with the glorious, bronzed, and chiseled torso of Mateo Cruz. He started coming for me, corralling me around the coffee table. I kept moving, circling away.

"Hmm, what could we do?" One side of his mouth ticked up. Rather than put me at ease, it held a world of dark promise that sent a tantalizing shiver down my spine, where it stalled between my legs. "How about we read some comic books together? There's a new issue where Wolverine—"

I shrieked and leaped. All it took was one mention of Wolverine, which for some reason really got Alpha's panties in a bunch. He had me on my back on the sofa, his fingers tickling up my ribs. Laughing so hard and loud, I squirmed and arched, trying my damnedest to get away. To no avail. His hard body caged me in, his heavy thighs pinning mine down.

"Stop!" I laugh-yelled.

He eased up, bracing one forearm by my head to hold his weight, the other hand splaying across my ribcage just under my breasts.

"You know what you've been doing to me in this outfit all night?"

I stared, soaking in the possessive, hot look he was giving me. I arched my neck, wanting his mouth there. He knew, leaning forward and scraping his teeth along the sensitive column.

"I know," I finally said. "We would've been here a lot earlier if I'd told you my secret."

"What secret?" His voice was all gruff and wolfy as he lifted up to hold my gaze.

I combed my fingers into his hair, grazing the nape of his neck the way he liked. "Why don't you take a look under my skirt and you'll find out." I bent my leg closest to the sofa back.

He went predatory still. It always amazed me how he could do that. Go so statue-like, as if he wasn't even breathing. I'd seen vampires do it, too. Right when they'd marked their blood host for the night.

His large hands with slender fingers, callused from working with the metal and the forge in his workshop, skimmed along the inside of my knee and up my thigh until it disappeared under my skirt. When those lovely, rough fingers found bare skin all the way up, his fire-gold eyes slipped closed and his chest rumbled with a dragon-deep growl. He licked his lips before he separated my folds with his middle finger, sliding down to my entrance then back up to my swollen nub where he circled lazily. I tightened my fingers in his hair and on his neck, breath coming quick.

That's when his eyes opened and pierced me with aching hunger. All wolf. All Alpha. He licked his lips again before he lowered his mouth almost to mine. But not quite.

"**I'm going to eat you up tonight**."

I whimpered at the gravelly voice of Alpha overtaking Mateo's. Then he pumped one finger inside me and bit my bottom lip before sweeping his tongue over the sting.

"**Would you like that**?"

Pumping my hips up to meet his too-slow stroking finger, I said, "Yes."

"**Tell me**."

I couldn't think straight with the languorous finger-fucking he was giving me. He slid a second finger inside, then demanded again, "**Tell me**."

Gripping his shoulders, I lifted my head, pressing a hard kiss to his perfect mouth. He let me stroke my tongue hard and deep, but he didn't quicken his pace at all. No. Not that son of a bitch. He enjoyed torturing me.

When I dropped my head in frustration, his fingers still moving too slow to get me there, he commanded again. "**Tell me what you want, baby, and I'll give it to you. I need to hear it tonight**."

Oh! Right. My brain caught up.

"I want you to eat me," I breathed against his lips. "Then I need you to fuck me hard."

His fingers were gone, my skirt was hiked up around my waist, and his hot mouth was between my legs, working my clit so fast an orgasm rocketed through my bones. I arched up, frozen in shock from the sudden, bone-melting climax.

I dug the heel of one foot into his back, since he'd tossed my leg over his shoulder, as I rode out my orgasm. He eased up with his tongue, rumbling a satisfying growl against my clit. At the moment my toes uncurled and my body went lax, he lifted up, then swept me back into his arms. Heading into the bedroom, he brushed a kiss against my temple.

"I like this skirt." Mateo was back.

I found it fascinating how the two of them switched off during sex. During those months he was under that curse, he'd fought for control with Alpha constantly. But now, they were symbiotic, living quite harmoniously in his headspace so he said. Mateo had also told me he didn't mind when Alpha wanted "out." When his wolf needed it, Mateo let him take control. Especially since they were really one and the same. And let me tell you, I didn't mind when Alpha came out to play. Not one bit.

I leaned up and bit his neck, then sucked hard.

"Mmm. Someone needs more."

"A lot more."

He tossed me on the bed and slid my miniskirt down my legs, his ravenous gaze raking over me. I didn't want to play anymore. I wanted him, now. I stripped my sweater over my head and unclasped my bra. While he worked on his jeans, I flung my bra aside and scooted up to the headboard. Once he'd pushed his jeans and boxers off and took hold of his hard cock, giving it a casual stroke before crawling up the bed, I bit my lip to keep from whimpering.

His mouth ticked up on one side. "You think you can keep quiet?"

I blinked, refusing to admit I couldn't. He knew I couldn't.

Rather than spread my legs and slide in between, he

maneuvered me quickly on my side with a large hand spread on my left hip, then he pressed up behind me. The hand on my hip eased down my outer thigh. He bent my leg and hooked it around his, which was slightly bent, opening me wide.

"**Look at me, Evie**."

Oh, fuck.

He cupped my cheek gently, turning my head toward him. I gripped his forearm then stared into his amber-gold eyes, flickering with supernatural fire.

"**Open your mouth, baby**."

When I did, he slid two fingers inside, stroking along my tongue once before using those fingers to circle the swollen nub between my legs. I clawed at his forearm and moaned. His eyes closed to slits, his heart hammering hard against my back where he pressed his chest to my spine.

"Make all the noise you want." He moved his hand away from my sex, taking his dick in hand to spread me further, slicking his head good before he sank inside.

I gasped, but he swallowed it with a fierce kiss, crushing his lips to mine and stroking his tongue deep. I didn't even try to hide my moans then, especially when he cupped one of my breasts, pinching my nipple lightly as he pumped his cock inside me.

"Yes," I hissed when he released my mouth but kept

his lips hovering over mine. I arched and rocked against him, trying to match his rhythm.

He buried his mouth against my neck. "**Feels so fucking good**."

My body hummed with pleasure. The sound of my wolf's voice, his hard body stroking me hard and deep, his rough hand caressing and squeezing, all of him pushing me toward ecstasy.

"Kiss me," I demanded.

He obeyed on a heavy groan, nipping and licking. When my moans escalated with the climb of another orgasm, he angled his mouth to swallow every sound, holding his dick inside me as my second peak rippled through me and around him.

Before I'd even come down, he growled out, "**I can't take it**."

Then I was on my stomach, my ass up, his hands spanning my hips and gripping hard as he pumped in with fierce thrusts. I clawed my nails into the covers, needing to hold onto something when Alpha let loose. The slapping of flesh against flesh, his masculine grunt every time he pushed to the hilt, and the sensation of my man thick and steel-hard for me was enough to send me into blissful oblivion.

"Tell me what you want," I taunted, even as he kept up his relentless thrusting and grunting.

"**You**," he practically roared, in a voice more beast than man. "**Always you**."

I clenched my muscles and squeezed, which sent him over the edge. He launched his body forward, almost crushing me beneath him. He held up enough so I could breathe as he speared me one last time, biting my shoulder and groaning through his release.

Both of us panting, we didn't say a word for a few moments. I slid one hand off the comforter toward his. Before I reached him, he covered mine, lacing our fingers together. He nuzzled into my neck, soft and sweet, his lips brushing gently.

"I love you, Evie."

The depth of Mateo's emotion vibrated in his voice. And though I'd heard the words many times before, it always filled me with the same euphoric pleasure. I'd never get overhearing those words from his lips. Just as I'd always feel the urgent need to remind him of the same.

"I love you, too."

In my young life as a witch, I'd seen the power of magic do miraculous things. A supernatural force that could bend metal, pound brick into dust, and crush the will of men into nothing. It was a power that could also do unimaginable good and create astounding beauty. Even so, it didn't come close to the overwhelming and mighty power of love.

It was like Christmas spirit. An intangible force you couldn't touch or hold in your hand. But it was a bone-deep feeling you knew and felt in the air every December. In the smiles of family, in the gathering of friends, in the kindness of strangers. It was real and powerful and true.

Just like the love that beat between our two hearts, winding us in a magical force all its own. Mateo pulled me into his arms and kissed the crown of my head.

"I have a little something for you."

I snickered, like the child I was. "You just gave me a big something."

Ignoring my dirty joke, he leaned over his side of the bed as I snuggled under the covers. He set a square box wrapped in Santa Claus wrapping paper on my stomach.

"Open it."

"Mateo." Sitting up with the sheet tucked between my arms and body to cover my boobs, I started ripping off the paper. "We're supposed to wait till Christmas."

"It's not your real present." Propped on his elbow, his beautiful, naked body was spread unashamedly on top of the covers. "This is something for both of us."

Totally confused, I made quick work of the paper and box, flinging the top off so fast I tore it. Mateo chuckled as I swished the red tissue paper out of the way to find two black T-shirts. I lifted the top one, a woman's fitted, long-sleeved tee in my size with Princess Leia saying, *I love you.* I laughed, because I already knew what the other extra-large T-shirt was. Yep. It was Han Solo replying, *I know.*

I squeezed them both to my bare breasts with a squeal. "I can't believe it."

His eyes smiled more than his mouth when he said, "I thought we could wear them together." He shrugged. "Christmas Eve."

Launching myself on top of him, he caught me and fell onto his back as I pecked kisses all over his face before gripping his finely sculpted jaw in both hands. "You are such a nerd."

"But you love me."

"More than ever."

He gripped my nape and pulled me down for a soft kiss. "Merry first Christmas."

"You're still too early."

"I want to tell you now."

"Merry first Christmas," I whispered back against his lips. "And to many more."

"Indeed."

Then we stopped talking with our mouths and wished each other merry one more time with our bodies. Later, as I drifted off to sleep, warm in his arms, I remember thinking it didn't matter what his real present was. This was already the best Christmas ever.

ROCKIN' AROUND THE HEXMAS TREE

Timeline: Takes place in December following* **Don't Hex and Drive.

CHAPTER 1

~ISADORA~

"I STILL DON'T UNDERSTAND why it's called White Elephant." Devraj stood in the foyer of his house holding two gifts brightly wrapped in red and green paper.

Though I'd moved in some of my clothes and my own toothbrush and other toiletries since we started dating in the spring, I still wasn't comfortable calling this *our* house. I mean, I loved the man more than I could even put into words, but our relationship wasn't even a year old. So I continued to think of it as his house, not ours, though he kept trying to convince me otherwise.

"I told you, the game has other names, too." I flicked off the kitchen lights and patted Archie on the head. "Be back later, baby."

He pranced in a circle before returning to his food bowl.

"Yeah, but I like Dirty Santa better." Devraj leaned against the door jamb, devouring me with his eyes.

Laughing, I crossed the living room and unplugged our Christmas tree lights. "I'll bet you do." I took one of the gifts from him, lifted onto my toes and planted a soft kiss on his lips. "Trust me. It's going to be fun."

"I always trust you." He laced his hand with mine after we closed the front door behind us. "You Americans just have weird names for things that don't make any sense."

"Like what?"

Since Devraj and I had been together, I'd learned so much about his past. I loved hearing about the many places he'd lived over the three hundred plus years he'd been alive. He was made by an ancient vampire in India centuries ago, but he'd lived all over the world. Some places longer than others. He'd spent a century in England, which is where he'd learned the English language. It wasn't surprising he favored lingo from the UK over that of America.

"Restroom, for one," he said, opening the wrought iron gate at the foot of his walkway. "You're not resting.

You're taking a piss. Is anyone actually going in there and lounging about and resting?"

I smiled up at him as we walked under the starlit sky. "What do they say in England?"

"Toilet," he answered with a snort. "Which is what it should be called, because that's what it is."

"What else?" I giggled.

"Flashlight. You're not flashing anything."

"Well, you could be. If you're turning it on and off really fast."

"Why would you do that? To speak in Morse code across a battlefield?" He squeezed my hand and tugged me closer to his side as we made the short walk to the house I'd lived in most of my life next door. "Again, it makes no sense."

"And what do you call a flashlight?"

"A torch."

"Now see, that makes no sense to me. Torches are made of fire."

"Ah, but torches were created to bring light. That was its purpose. It's much more accurate than flashlight."

"In your opinion." I let go of his hand as we walked up the porch and I opened the door.

Classic Frank Sinatra holiday music crooned from the living room. Clara swished through with a platter of hors d'oeuvres, wearing a green dress with a black sash, the skirt flaring at her knees, and a matching green elf hat.

"Hey, y'all!" She set the platter on a side table and rushed over to take our presents. "I'll take the White Elephant gifts, and you guys go get a drink."

Masculine laughter echoed from the kitchen where I could see Nico and Mateo drinking some kind of cocktail. Amber liquid, so probably whiskey. Mateo was Evie's boyfriend and Nico was his cousin. He'd started hanging with our family regularly since his only relative here in New Orleans was Mateo, and he fitted in quite well. Especially now that he and Violet were opening a tattoo shop together.

"There you are." Evie popped up and handed us each a tumbler of a white drink over crushed ice. She was wearing a cute black dress and a red Santa hat.

"JJ's eggnog?" I asked excitedly, already putting the glass to my lips.

She smiled. "Of course! He has his own thing tonight, but I got him to make a batch for us."

"Sweet heaven," I whispered before taking another sip of the sugary cinnamon and fiery whiskey concoction.

Devraj leaned over close to my ear, "That's what I say every time we're in bed."

I almost choked on my drink then shot him a glare. "Behave," I whispered.

He simply smiled and strolled over to the guys. Livvy bustled out with a tray of chips and dip. Looked like that spinach artichoke with jalapeno cheese that Jules made. My mouth started watering.

"Yum. Can I help, Jules?"

Jules untied her apron and tossed it on the counter, then carried in some bacon-wrapped shrimp and jalapenos. "I think we've got it, Iz. Okay, everyone!" She said as she passed back into the living room. "Grab a plate and dig in."

Even before Mom and Dad retired to Switzerland, we'd always had a casual family Christmas party where we gathered in the living room and ate nothing but fatty appetizers and high-calorie drinks then played our Christmas games. Mom and Dad weren't going to make it this holiday, but they'd promised to come soon.

Livvy and I had recently visited and realized that they were truly enjoying their retirement years together. It wasn't that they didn't love New Orleans or us. They'd both been born and raised here, then raised all of us here too. It was just that they were truly loving their new, quiet life together without all the troubles of the world weighing down on them. So we didn't blame them for not wanting to make the big trek home for all the holidays.

"No, ma'am!" yelled Jules from the makeshift buffet table she'd set up. "He cannot join the party, Violet."

Violet had her rooster Fred tucked under her arm. He was wearing a red bowtie with tiny green Christmas trees on them.

"But look at how cute he looks," she whined.

"Everyone," said Jules cheerfully to the room. "Look at how adorable Fred is." Then she turned back to Violet. "Now go put him outside."

"Ugh." Violet turned back toward the kitchen. We all heard the back patio door open and slam.

"She's got a bit of a temper, doesn't she?" Mateo said casually to Evie.

"Yeah, but she gets over it quickly."

Nico's gaze was on the kitchen where she'd left, his green eyes gleaming unnaturally bright. A tingle of magic sizzled in a radius around him. His wolf was present. Interesting.

Nico always seemed so calm and quiet, but his broodiness had a little edge tonight. It probably was because it was obvious he wanted something with my crazy sister Violet, but either she hadn't noticed or she wasn't having it.

We all settled with plates of delicious appetizers and filled our bellies. Violet returned and as always, was already over Jules bouncing Fred from the party. She settled on the ottoman after she'd gotten a plate.

"Okay, guys. First game!" called out Clara after we'd

all had time to eat. She was always the official game host of the family Christmas party.

"What's this one called?" asked Livvy.

"Drink While You Grinch."

"Hell yeah." Violet popped off the ottoman and rushed into the kitchen, calling, "I need more eggnog! Wait for me, Clara!"

"No need," said Clara, sitting in the center of one of the sofas. "The rules are super simple."

They'd pushed the chairs from the corner sitting area to form a big square surrounding the coffee table along with the sofa and loveseat.

"This is easy to learn," said Clara. "When it's your turn, you have to drink until you can think of something about Christmas you hate. And the trick is, you can't repeat what anyone else has already said."

"I'll go first!" I called out, knowing the game would get harder with each person.

"Of course you will, lightweight," said Livvy teasingly. It was true, I wasn't a heavy drinker like them.

Arching an eyebrow at Livvy, I started to drink, giving myself one big gulp before stopping. I already had something to say. "I hate the long lines while shopping."

"Everyone hates that," said Evie.

"Exactly. But I said it first, and now you've got to come up with something else."

"Your turn, Devraj," said Clara. "We're going clockwise."

Violet rushed back in and took her place, folding cross-legged on the ottoman. "What did I miss?"

"You have to drink till you think of something you hate about Christmas. No repeats. Iz said she hates shopping lines," Evie explained succinctly.

"Got it." Violet nodded.

Devraj started to gulp down his eggnog, and all I could do was lust over the way the muscular cords and Adam's apple worked in his neck as he drank it down. You'd think that I might get used to his masculine beauty after being together so many months, but I totally wasn't. Sometimes, all it took was a tilted smile or a smoldering look or catching sight of him drinking eggnog to get me all hot and bothered. It was ridiculous. But I just couldn't help it. Devraj was a stunning specimen of manhood.

He stopped drinking and licked the excess off his lips. I squeezed my thighs together at the hot sensation between my legs.

"I hate pop Christmas albums that always come out this time of year."

"Damn. You took mine," said Nico.

Violet grinned. "You better start thinking of another one, wolfie."

Nico shot her an electric look. His wolf was definitely in the building.

"My turn." Clara took three sips and stopped. "I hate that Christmas is the only time most people feel compelled to give to charities. Specifically the homeless."

Violet rolled her eyes. "Lots of people give to charities and the homeless all year long."

"Really? When was the last time you helped down at the homeless shelter?" Clara asked accusingly.

"I don't need to, because my twin sister donates double the normal person. So I'm covered."

"That's not the way it works, Vi."

"We can't all be as good as you, sis," Violet added truthfully with not a hint of menace.

"I'm not *that* good," whispered Clara.

"My turn!" shouted Evie from on top of Mateo's lap.

And so it went. We did two rounds before we ran out of things to say, because truthfully we were down to nitpicky things that were getting really silly, and we knew we couldn't go on. Because honestly, there really wasn't anything serious to hate about the holidays. More like inconveniences. Except for Livvy's last one.

"It's true though," said Livvy. "I seriously loathe

anything pumpkin flavored. And who wants to drink pumpkin? It's just gross."

"Okay, guys!" Clara hopped up and hustled over to the Christmas tree. "Time for White Elephant."

She gathered everyone's presents and hauled them to the center coffee table in a few trips. Everyone took a quick bathroom break or refilled their drinks then got settled on the sofas and chairs again. I stayed put, snuggled into the warmth of Devraj while he combed his fingers through the hair hanging over my shoulder.

Clara raced into the kitchen and returned with a bowl holding folded up pieces of paper.

"I'm glad we have more people this year, because that makes it more fun."

I turned my head up to Devraj's ear and whispered, "I'm glad too."

He gave me that heart-melting smile and kissed my lips. It was closed-mouth but so slow and lingering that I knew he was making promises for later tonight. I caught his gaze dropping to the hem of my dress which was shorter than usual, showing a little more leg than normal.

"Pick, Isadora," said Clara, standing in front of us.

I pulled my number. "Two." I showed Devraj. "What did you get?"

"Nine. That was lucky."

"It is!" Clara agreed excitedly. "You'll be the last to

go." She moved on to Evie and Mateo then said, "Now remember. You can steal the same gift no more than three times, y'all. So the third person to steal something gets that present." She took the last paper in the bowl then asked, "So who's one?"

Nico raised his hand with a crooked smile, then he leaned forward and picked a fairly big rectangular box. Ripping the paper off, he held up a deluxe foot spa.

He chuckled. "I could actually use this."

Violet rolled her eyes. "Yeah, because your feet are aching so much from sitting on a stool in bars, singing."

He didn't mind her snarky mouth, it seemed. "You know damn well I've been working on the final renovations of the shop nonstop. So I have been on my feet more than usual. Besides, some of us like to relax and enjoy simple pleasures." He grinned before he swigged his whiskey.

She didn't have anything to say to that.

"Number two," called Clara.

"That's me." I leaned forward and plucked a small present wrapped in silvery snowflake paper.

I unwrapped the unmarked box, opened it and pulled back the tissue paper. Seeing a small gold cord, I lifted out the prettiest ornament I'd ever seen. It was encased in clear plastic wrap to protect it, since it was made of white ceramic glass. There were star-shaped cut-outs in the glass where I could see a myriad of herbs and dried flowers inside. Through the plastic covering, I could barely smell sage and lemongrass along with an unfamiliar perfume scenting the interior. I could even see dried pansy petals inside.

"This is so pretty," I gushed, admiring the painted scenery on the white ceramic. It was of two little girls playing in the snow, a dog dancing around them in front of an old porch. There was a rooster standing on the porch. I laughed. "This looks like Fred."

"What! Let me see." Violet reached out her hand.

"You can see it, but it's mine."

Violet smiled, while looking at the ornament. "It *does* look like Fred. Look how cute!" She showed Livvy.

"I thought so, too," said Clara, grinning widely. "I found it in a shop last month."

Violet shared a look with Clara. As twins, they connected on another level than the rest of us a lot of the time, even though they were polar opposites in personality. It seemed Clara had gotten this one, thinking Violet would like the rooster.

"Give it back," I told Violet. "The little dog looks sort of like Archie, too."

She arched a superior eyebrow at me as she passed it over. "You can have it back. For now."

I tucked it in the tissue paper and playfully hid it under the hem of my skirt.

She laughed, then Jules went. She immediately

snatched up a square present and opened it to reveal a set of eight beautiful stemless wine glasses.

"Oh, wow. What a surprise." She deadpanned with a smirk. "I think I'll keep these."

"Jules," Livvy snapped. "You can't take your own gift."

"Who says?" She narrowed her gray-blue eyes. "I needed a new set."

While they squabbled, Violet hopped up and came for me. "My turn!" She held out her hand. "Give it, Izzy. I want that ornament."

Huffing, I pulled it out and handed it over. "I can't believe you're going to steal that, knowing I'm the plant lover and herbalist in the family."

"Exactly. You could make yourself one of these. Besides, I put up a little tree in the shop, and I need ornaments."

"You're not even open yet," I pointed out.

"The energy of a room is always important, Iz," Violet explained. "And I want good vibes and cheer for Empress Ink."

The game rolled on. Mateo ended up stealing Nico's foot bath, so Nico stole Evie's bottle of Salted Caramel Crown Royal. Then Livvy stole the foot bath from Mateo, and he took the Crown back from Nico and handed it back to Evie. Then finally it was Devraj's turn.

He turned to me with that heart-melting look and traced a finger along my jaw before he hopped up and walked over to Violet.

"The ornament, please, darling."

"How can you possibly sound so utterly charming while stealing a gift from me?"

He shrugged and held out his hand, curling his fingers in the international sign for *gimme*.

Pouting, she did, and he waltzed over and placed it in my lap with that bone-melting smile that always undid me.

With a huff, Violet walked over to Evie. "Hand over the Crown. I need it now."

Mateo growled.

"Oh, don't start with me. Blame it on the vampire. He stole my ornament."

When Mateo, or rather Alpha, his inner wolf, glared with yellow-gold eyes at Devraj, my man simply smiled and pulled me into his lap.

"Whatever my girl wants, she gets."

"Thank you, Dev," I whispered, pecking him on the lips.

Livvy drew everyone into another drinking game, but I didn't move from Dev's lap, perfectly content to watch and laugh at their antics. To be honest, I was ready to get home and be alone with him.

So when the party started to wind down, I stood and tugged on Dev's hand.

"Thank you, Jules, and Clara, for doing all the heavy lifting for the party."

"Of course." Jules smiled contentedly from her perch on a chair with a glass of red wine, watching Violet and Livvy argue over something in their game. "Glad y'all came."

She stood and gave Dev a hug then me. Dev opened his mouth to say something, then seemed to change his mind, offering a simple "goodnight" before we left through the front door.

"What were you going to ask her?" I looped my arm through his as we made our way through the wrought iron gate.

"I wanted to ask why she didn't invite Ruben, but then realized it's really not my place."

"Ruben isn't really family."

"Isadora." The way he said my name in that deep rumble sent a shiver over my skin. "You know as well as everyone with eyes in their heads that those two care for each other."

For a moment, I didn't say anything, then decided to confess a little. "Yes. Something happened between them years ago. But Jules won't tell any of us. I think you're right. They seem to still care a great deal."

"Ruben won't tell me anything either. But I know he

wants her. I'm not sure what will finally make him realize that he's wasting time trying to pretend he's ever going to get over her." We walked in silence for a minute before he asked, "Do you think she'd ever give him a chance?"

I had to consider that for a minute. "Jules is the most guarded of all my sisters. Violet seems pretty damn stubborn, but Jules is more so. Since what happened between Jules and Ruben is a mystery, it's hard to say." Glancing up at Devraj's beautiful face, gilded in silver from the moonlight, I added, "But I suppose there's always hope."

He gazed down with love in his eyes, reaching his arm around my waist to pull me close, hip to hip, as we walked along. "There's always hope, my heart."

CHAPTER 2

~DEVRAJ~

ONCE BACK AT THE HOUSE, I plugged in the lights on the tree and checked on Archie. He wagged his little tail from his fluffy bed but didn't get up. Returning to the living room, I found Isadora lifting her new ornament from the box and unwrapping the clear plastic wrap around it. She smelled the aromatic potpourri inside through the cut-outs. Watching her place the ornament on the tree, a zing of warmth pummeled through me. That warmth suddenly transformed into something much hotter. A gut-punch of searing lust.

She looked like an angel in that dress, the white lights from the tree glowing on her fair skin. An angel I wanted to strip naked and fuck. This was nothing new. I couldn't get enough of this woman. No matter how many times and ways I took her sweet body, I always wanted more. Something pounded hard at me now, skyrocketing my desire to desperate heights.

What was it that had set me off? The tilt of her slender neck, exposed with her blond hair piled in a messy twist on her head? Perhaps those long bare legs in that short dress? Or maybe just her scent that acted like an aphrodisiac, even from across the room. Sweet floral, spicy herb, and warm woman wafted over me, jerking on my cock as if she'd wrapped her hand around it.

Obeying my need, I strolled over to her, stopping right behind her as she admired the tree. I grazed my nose along the curve from her neck to shoulder, my dick already rock-hard.

"Take off your clothes, Isadora."

She flinched, surely detecting the gravelly tone of my voice, knowing the monster that lived inside me was riding me hard. Vampires were seductive creatures but monsters nonetheless. We used our beauty to lure prey closer.

Isadora knew that I'd never harm her. I'd slit my own throat before I ever laid a hand on her in violence, but there were moments when the monster wanted satisfaction. Dominance and aggression ruled me at times like these. The beast wanted his woman's body and blood.

She peered over her shoulder, recognizing my need was grave and deep. Sliding down the zipper along the side of her dress, she let the straps fall off her shoulder and pushed the dress to the floor. Her pulse tripped faster, humming in the air and making my incisors ache.

I didn't even need to feel with my tongue to know that my fangs were fully descended, throbbing to sink into her silky skin. I refused to touch her yet, knowing that I'd be inside her the second I did. A feverish craving had overtaken me the moment I walked into this room and saw her silhouetted by the glow of the tree. I couldn't explain it. But I knew one thing. I had to feed it.

"Take off everything," I commanded.

Gooseflesh pebbled her skin. She remained facing away from me as she unhooked her bra and dropped it to the floor. Then slowly peeled her lace panties down her long legs. Before I said another word, she turned, sank to her knees and started grappling with my belt buckle.

Her hands were shaking as she whipped open my belt and unzipped my pants. Pulling out my hard dick, she had her lips wrapped around the head in seconds, those deep green eyes staring up at me.

"Fuck, baby," I whispered, watching her swallow me down, taking me to the back of her throat.

I pulled my sweater over my head and tossed it aside. Combing my fingers into her hair, I cradled her head with one hand and her nape with the other, urging her to take more of me. She clutched my thighs, blunt nails digging into the muscle, cheeks hollowed out while she sucked me hard.

"That's it. Suck me good. Show me how much you want it."

At my firm grip and shallow thrusting, her pupils dilated full black, only a rim of green glittering by the tree lights. I skated my thumb up her jaw to shape her lower lip as she sucked me down. My cock was scorching hot and throbbing, yearning to pound deeper. But I knew she couldn't take me all of the way.

Her eyes slipped closed as she squirmed, her hand slipping between her legs to rub her clit.

"Is my pussy wet for me?" I growled, that sweet, spicy scent filling my nostrils. "Fuck yes, it is."

She moaned again, the slick sound of her wetness as she stroked herself driving me mad while she bobbed on my cock. Her sucking wasn't easing this burning need, it was ramping it higher. I felt like I would erupt in flames if I didn't bury myself deep inside her. And yet, that scent.

I let out a string of curses as I thrust one last time

and pulled out when she gagged, her eyeliner running. Hands under her arms, I hoisted her up against the wall. I shoved her straight up the wall, high above me, an easy feat for my vampire strength. All I knew was that I needed to taste her. *Now.*

She immediately draped her thighs over my shoulders, her hands digging into my hair while she rocked her pussy closer.

Groaning, I opened my mouth on her silky lips, licking and sucking like a starving man. With one hand on her ass, fingertips digging into the cleft, I rubbed a circle around her entrance with the index and middle finger of the other.

"Devraj," she begged, rocking her hips in circles as I lapped at her clit. "Please, please."

I sank my fingers inside her nice and slow. Too slow. She whimpered in frustration.

"More. Shit, what's happening? I need you."

I clamped my lips around her clit and thrust my fingers deep. Her inner muscles clamped with her quickening orgasm, pulsing around my fingers as I nibbled on her clit. She was still rocking her hips, her pussy against my face when I eased her down the wall into my arms and lined my cock at her entrance. She wrapped her long legs around my hips.

"I want to feel that again, sweetheart," I murmured

into her ear. "Need to feel you come on my dick this time." Then I thrust deep.

"Anything you want," she whispered into my neck, licking up the side. "Fuck me hard, Dev."

"Whatever my queen commands."

Holding her ass in both hands, I pounded into her, the sensation of her tight heat, her intoxicating scent, her submissive body driving me toward a fire-bright peak. Dipping my head to her shoulder, I skated my sharpened fangs up the slope, not breaking her skin.

"Oh, God! Fuck me! Bite me!" She clenched her fist in my hair and tilted her head back, exposing her throat, my dick swelled bigger as I slid in long, deep glides, pounding her hard with each thrust.

"Isadora," I growled before I sank my fangs into her throat.

An agonizing groan vibrated from her to me or the other way around. I wasn't sure. We were nothing but sizzling bliss, an erotic melding of sensation and desire catapulting toward an explosive climax.

My chest vibrated with the guttural groan and pleasure of her blood seeping down my throat, of her tight pussy milking me in a pulsing orgasm. I didn't want to come yet, staving off the end with dizzying concentration. Our flesh slapped as I pistoned harder, deeper, fucking her with insatiable need.

I had no idea where this flaming desire had come

from, but I knew it wouldn't be over until I spilled my cum inside of her. On that very thought, my dick throbbed with the first wave of a mind-melting orgasm.

Pulling my mouth from her throat, I tipped my head back and roared as I fucked her through every hot spurt. Then she was coming again, squeezing me so hard I saw dark spots at the edge of my vision. Burying my mouth into her hair, I pressed a kiss before sweeping to her temple then her forehead then her cheek till I found her mouth.

Tasting her with soft strokes of my tongue, I moaned again, my dick spurting one more time inside of her. My thighs shook with the intensity of our coupling, making me realize my pants were still halfway down my legs. When I pulled back and looked into her eyes, I saw the same shocked surprise.

"What the hell was that?" she asked, panting so hard her breath blew the loose strands of hair trailing in front of her eyes.

"I don't know," I chuckled, shaking my head, tucking her loose hair over one ear. "Guess we both just needed it."

"We made love yesterday morning," she reminded me.

"Indeed." I brushed my mouth sweetly across hers in a teasing sweep. "So very long ago."

She smiled against my lips, loving my teasing. "Take

me to bed." She anchored her arms more tightly around my neck. "To *sleep*." she emphasized.

I eased out of her, relishing the soft gasp she made then set her on her feet so I could pull my pants back up. Once done, I swept her back into my arms.

"I don't know why you're fussing at me. You were the one who couldn't wait to suck my cock."

"Devraj!" She hit me playfully on the chest then smiled. "Can you blame me? It's a perfect cock."

I grinned as I carried her into our bedroom, tossed her on the bed, and fell on top of her.

"I'm supposed to be the charming one, my love." I swept her hair away from her cheeks so I could see her whole beautiful face.

She laughed. "Calling your cock perfect is charming?"

"To me it is. Just like this face is perfect." I swept light kisses from one side to the other. "And this neck." I coasted my lips down her throat, licked the two puncture wounds where I'd bitten her, then kept going. "And these breasts." I circled one nipple with my tongue till it was taut and jutting up for more attention, then I sucked it hard.

Isadora squirmed beneath me, her hips rocking up on instinct.

"This breast too." I trailed my tongue from one tip

down the slope and up to the other, then suckled her till she was squirming even more.

"Dev," she whispered, cupping my head to hold me there.

"But I haven't even mentioned this perfect torso." I continued kissing down one side of her ribcage then her navel. "Or the most heavenly, perfect pussy I've ever tasted." I lightly licked my tongue around her swollen clit, not caring that our juices were mingled. That scent of her is what drew me back down.

She whimpered softly and pressed my head closer to her pussy. I gave her a brief suckle then lifted my head to peer up at her. Her hair had fallen, her makeup was smudged, her eyes were glassy with drugged desire. So fucking beautiful.

"I thought you wanted to sleep." I swept my tongue out and flicked her clit, still holding her gaze.

She jumped then whimpered, biting her bottom lip. "One more time, Dev," she whispered.

"As my queen commands."

CHAPTER 3

~ISADORA~

I SAT at the breakfast table eating strawberry yogurt while Archie ate his bowl of breakfast kibble as well. My mind kept wandering to last night. I smiled, loving how we couldn't get enough of each other like it had been at the very start of our relationship.

Not that our desire had dimmed. But we'd become more content just to be in each other's company, snuggled together on the sofa watching a movie or drinking wine on the back patio while Archie ran around the yard. As long as we were together, that humming sensation of rightness, of contentment and satisfaction wove between us both.

But last night. *Jeesh.*

I could barely think straight when he came up behind me. All I knew is I needed to taste him or I'd go mad.

He'd already left for the day to meet Ruben on whatever vampire task he had. I quickly finished up and let Archie into the backyard before I walked to our shop on the corner, Mystic Maybelle's.

"Good morning," I called to Clara who was on a step ladder straightening some new metaphysical books we'd gotten in this week.

"Morning," she beamed over her shoulder before climbing down. "How was your night?"

For a second, I wondered if it was plastered all over my face that I'd gotten my brains fucked out last night.

"You mean the party?" My voice was a little high.

She laughed, a sweet infectious sound. "Of course." She narrowed her gaze on me with a wicked gleam. "What did you think I meant?"

"The party was fabulous." I zipped behind the counter and petted Z where he was curled up in his pink bed. "You and Jules did a great job as always."

"Thank you very much." She sashayed behind the counter and grabbed her wrist wallet. "I've got an order to pick up at the Queen of Tarts if you don't mind watching the store for a few minutes."

"Of course not. Did we get any new inventory?"

"Just one box. Right here." She tugged it from underneath the counter, then headed out the door, jingling the bell overhead.

Clara was mighty chipper this morning. That was nothing new, but my instincts—my witchy instincts—were telling me something was a little off with her.

I opened the box to find some new quill pen and ink holders. Though not metaphysical obviously, we did have clients that enjoyed whimsical literary things as well. As a matter of fact, I thought of buying the green one for myself.

Once I'd catalogued the new inventory into my online bookkeeping program, I closed the box up and set it aside for Clara to display as she wished. She had the eye for design. I was just the caretaker behind the scenes. The store's one customer strolled around the shelves.

"Can I help you find anything?" I asked.

"No, thank you. Just looking around."

Thankful to return to my own thoughts, I went to the window display and checked on the white Christmas lights. Clara insisted that they be plugged in night and day since Thanksgiving, so we'd had to change out a string already. Nope, everything looked as pretty as when she'd first made the display.

She'd created a tier of crystal balls, the glass domes and shimmering white marble bases sparkled alongside enlarged prints of our favorite Tarot cards with gold filigree and silver detailing. The cards were propped on easels of varying heights. She'd even enlarged one Empress card in honor of Violet and Nico's new shop Empress Ink. Along with the faux snow she'd sprinkled over it all and the white lights, it looked absolutely beautiful.

Movement caught my eye across the street. Clara was exiting Queen of Tarts talking to someone behind her. She carried a large white bakery box and right behind her was Henry, the grim who'd helped us capture the vampires behind that blood trafficking ring a few months ago.

I liked Henry, but he was an odd one. Hell, he was a grim reaper. That should explain it all. They were all odd…and secretive.

Clara babbled about something happily as they walked side by side across the street toward us. He carried a white bakery box as well.

As usual, he was saying nothing, just listening and watching as they crossed. He moved in front of a car before she crossed, glaring at the driver who seemed a bit frustrated at the pedestrians crossing. The driver held up both hands in surrender while Henry glowered at him and Clara was safe back on the sidewalk.

I hurried to the door and held it open as they carried the boxes in, Clara still chattering.

"But honestly, it was the Victorians who started it all. The true elevation of baking to an artform."

"What the heck did you buy?" I asked, staring at the two big boxes. "Are you having another party I don't know about?"

"Yes!" exclaimed Clara. "It's our annual High Tea Book Club Christmas party tonight, and I wanted to go all out. Miss Abigail hasn't been feeling well lately, and she just adores pastry. I wanted to make her feel better."

She set her box on the counter and popped open the top.

"So we've got some Danish pastries with drizzled icing, cream-stuffed French pastries with almond slivers on top, blueberry and apple strudel."

She closed the box and pushed it aside and took the other from Henry.

"Thank you." She beamed at him, and I swear the top of the grim's high cheekbones flushed pink. "And we have pear and cinnamon mince pies, some mini quiches with spinach and mushroom, and some little chicken pies."

"Wow," I exclaimed, staring at the pastry feast. "You might send them into gluten shock."

"Don't worry. I'm making some salad, too."

As if that would help.

"You remember Henry, don't you?" she asked pleasantly.

I didn't remember him from the night Devraj had rescued me, but we'd met after that whole ugly ordeal.

"Hi, Henry. It's good to see you again."

He merely nodded. Man of few words, that one. His dark aura had pushed through the door right as he'd walked in, but I'd immediately sucked light energy from the air and wove a shield around myself to prevent the effects of his grimness.

There was little known about the grims, except that they all exuded an aura that tapped into a person's darkest hungers and desires. For those who enjoyed diving into sinful cravings, it had a heady effect. Thus the reason Ruben had hired him; to hang close to his vampire den. It was good for the blood host business.

"Henry just happened to be stopping in the bakery at the same time as me and offered to help me carry this load back over here."

That flush of pink darkened, which was extremely noticeable against his pale skin. Henry was an element of contrasts. Coal-black eyes and hair, super fair skin, broodily silent, and yet apparently helpful in offering to carry pastries. Of course, the way he looked at my sister explained why.

"I'd better go," he said, his voice deep and husky.

"Oh! Not yet." She grasped his forearm. "Let me show you around our shop."

His gaze dropped to her hand, and I was positive

that Henry Blackwater had zero interest in our metaphysical shop. Yet, he nodded all the same.

The other roaming customer came up to the register, so I rang up her books and pack of Oracle cards.

"Thank you," she said when I handed over her bag and receipt.

"You're welcome. Happy holidays."

When she exited with a jingle of the bell over the door, I resumed my observation of Clara as she dragged the grim around the store, pointing out all of our different items on display.

"Those don't actually work though," he said, pointing to our display of herbal teas and potions, all of which were infused with mine or Clara's magic.

As an Aura, she could inject positive energy into anything, including herbs among other things. With my Conduit magic, I could pour healing magic into others.

We labeled each tea and sachet of herbs—some were drinkable, some were meant for burning or simply hanging in the house—for how they helped. Some were to help with stress reduction, headaches, high blood pressure, sleep deprivation, and even warding off negative energy.

"Of course they do," Clara assured him.

"Even that one?" he stared down at her, skepticism in his voice.

I tried to see what he was pointing to. Clara removed her hand from his arm and twisted them behind her back.

"Well, yes and no," she answered rather shyly. Not like Clara.

Normally, I'd stay out of other people's conversations. To be honest, I preferred living in my own bubble and venturing out only when absolutely necessary. But my curiosity was killing me over here. And I was a little irritated that Henry would doubt our magical abilities.

"What is he asking about, Clara?"

They both turned, wide-eyed like two children caught doing something naughty.

"The love potion," she said, her own cheeks flushing pink now.

Ahhh. Now that makes sense.

"Well, *you'd* have to tell him all about that," I said, coming from around the counter and leaning my back against it and crossing my arms. "That's your area of expertise."

Henry's dark gaze was fixed on her now. He stuffed his hands in his jean pockets, waiting.

"It's not actually a love potion," she clarified.

Oh, this was going to be fun.

"Then what is it?" he asked, that deep voice resonating even darker.

She cleared her voice and turned to straighten some books on a shelf behind her.

"We can't really make people fall in love," she emphasized as if that were a silly idea.

"Well, that's what it's called."

"That's because it sounds better than what it truly is." She paused, finishing up straightening the books before turning back to him. "A lust potion."

A blazing wave radiated in the room. Grim magic. All magic had a signature, felt a certain way. Some could feel like a blast of power or a tingling along the skin. But Henry's just felt like…fire.

I watched the two of them stare at each other for what felt like an eternity but was probably about fifteen seconds, then Henry took a step back.

"I need to be going." He turned abruptly for the door.

"Thank you for helping me carry the pastries," said Clara.

He stopped in the open doorway, his hand white-knuckled on the frame as he turned his head to look over his shoulder. His dark eyes glinted with an edginess, then he gave her a tight nod before leaving.

Clara exhaled a heavy sigh.

I laughed. "Whoa. So what's going on between you and Henry Blackwater?"

She stared dazedly at the space where he was standing. "Hmm?"

"You and Henry," I clarified. "You know, the guy who was just here practically drooling all over you."

She scoffed. Pulling her waist-length hair over one shoulder, she started to braid it. "He wasn't drooling."

"Really? What's that puddle over there for?"

She actually looked. I laughed.

"Isadora. You are not allowed to tease me."

"Why not?"

"Because," she huffed, finishing her long braid and removing a ponytail holder from her wrist and tying it off. "Because if he doesn't feel the same way I do, I'll just die."

"Oh, come on, Clara. Can't you tell he likes you?"

She shook her head, walking over behind the counter and picking up the box of new inventory. "Did you log all of this?"

"Yes. And no, you're not changing the subject. Surely you can feel what he feels about you."

She plunked down the box by a display table. "That's just it. I *can't*."

She looked at me with exasperation. Yes, Clara was exasperated. I'm not sure I'd seen that look on her face in maybe forever.

"I don't understand. You're the most gifted Aura in

New Orleans. Surely you can sense his emotions when he's around you. You'd *know* how he felt."

"I'm telling you, Iz, I can't. It's so frustrating." Then she propped both hands on her hips, staring at the display like it had offended her. "And also," her voice softened, "so absolutely wonderful."

"Sorry? I'm so confused now."

"It's like this," she turned to me. "I can sense any emotion of any person I've ever met the moment they're within twenty yards of me. But Henry? I've never been able to read him. Not once. He's the only person that's ever happened with."

"What about his grim aura vibes? Doesn't he give you the darker feelings?"

"No," she answered easily. "Not at all. It's like we cancel each other out or something."

"So you don't feel anything at all?"

"Well," she smiled at me before bending to pull out some of the feather quill pens, "I wouldn't say that."

"This is rather fascinating."

"Isn't he?" she said dreamily, decorating the display table.

"That's not what I said."

"What?" She glanced wide-eyed at me.

"Never mind. Get back to daydreaming. I'm going to work in the office a while."

She didn't answer but turned to look out the door

again, a goofy smile on her face. I'm pretty sure that's how I looked last night right before I fell asleep. Perhaps I looked a bit more satisfied than she did.

❄

I CHOPPED the shallots and mushrooms for the Chicken Marsala I was cooking for dinner. Devraj had come home and changed clothes to do his yoga in the yard as he did every afternoon.

By the time I'd cooked the chicken breasts and added the rest of the ingredients to simmer and put the pot of water on to boil for the pasta, he was walking into the door from the back patio.

"Have some good yoga time?" I asked, looking up from the stove.

Then it hit me. A jarring wave of lust sizzled along my skin as I watched him swagger into the kitchen shirtless in his gray joggers and hair in a bun. I'd seen him like this a hundred times, but today, I wanted to rip those joggers off with my teeth and sink to my knees and suck him again like last night.

"My love," he said softly with a little raspy darkness, his eyes glinting silver. "It isn't wise to look at me that way. Unless you're sending me an invitation."

I couldn't speak. I left the stove and reached him in

three long strides. Since the weather had turned cold, I was wearing more tights and cardigans rather than my billowy dresses. It aggravated the hell out of me right now because if I was wearing a dress, I could climb on top of him and slip him inside me right this damn second.

A rush of hunger pummeled me with ferocious need. I had my mouth on his and my hand in his joggers in three seconds.

He groaned at my grip, already hard and throbbing harder with each stroke. My thumb swiped the pre-cum at his crown, and I whimpered at his readiness.

Still kissing me, he managed to shove off his pants then yanked off my long cardigan. He gripped the front of my camisole top and ripped it in half, my breasts popping free since the bra was built into the camisole. Well, what was left of it.

He opened his hot mouth on one nipple and sucked and licked and groaned, fighting to get my tights off. The whole time, I was squeezing and clawing him like mad too.

"For fuck's sake," he growled, grabbing me roughly and bending me over the kitchen table.

I arched for him, needing friction on my pussy with wild desperation. "Devraj. Need you. Please, please, please."

He'd grabbed the top of my tights and panties and

jerked them down to my ankles then plunged his thick cock inside me.

"Oh, God, yes! Just like that."

He growled, his hand sliding up my spine to the nape of my neck where he gripped firmly. "Always so wet for me, sweetheart. My eager little pussy."

"Yes, yes!" I arched my spine, thrusting my ass higher, my palms flat on the kitchen table.

"Spread wider for me." His husky tone was tinged with strain, not his usual silkiness during sex. He was feeling this same unquenchable need, driving us both like a jackhammer through bedrock. "Wider." He reached underneath and slapped my pussy.

That got me moving. I jerked one leg free of my tangled panties and yoga pants and spread my legs, stretching my body farther over the table. My nipples grazed the cold wood with each deep thrust.

"There you go," he crooned.

His free hand dipped around my hip and between my legs where he stroked my swollen nub with light circles, his other hand still around my nape.

I made a frustrated sound. "Harder."

He lifted his hand away, slapping my pussy lips lightly again. I jumped and almost came on the spot, my inner walls clenching around his thrusting cock.

"I'll give it to you when I'm ready, love. You just relax and take it."

I stretched my arms wider on the cold surface, all the sensations driving me higher. Cold hard wood beneath me, caressing my tight nipples. His hot, thick dick thrusting, his pelvis grinding and knocking me against the table. His rough fingers playing too softly around my sensitized clit.

I needed friction. Needed it hard. Needed it now!

Still frustrated, all while being so turned on I couldn't think straight, I pushed back with my hips, trying to get him to go harder, faster.

He chuckled. "Trying to top from the bottom, my love?"

That light slap against my pussy came again, shocking me with a wave of pleasure-pain. "What did I tell you?" He impaled me deep and held, not moving. "Be patient, sweetheart."

His gentle words were in total contradiction with the wild gruffness of his voice. He sounded like a feral beast coaxing his prey into a cage. I was ready and willing to climb into his cage. I'd do anything to get him to fuck me rough and senseless.

"Please, baby," I begged, squirming, needing him to move. But he'd gone stone still.

He leaned forward, covering me with his broad chest, the blanket of fiery heat against my back adding to the titillating sensations of contrast. He wrapped one forearm around my shoulder and scooped his hand down to grip my breast. The other hand remained between my legs, circling my throbbing nub with agonizingly slow, soft sweeps. He nuzzled into my hair.

"What do you need, my love?"

I moaned.

"Tell me," he urged, mounding my breast with his large hand then tweaking the nipple.

My sex clinched in response.

He hissed in a breath, his cock swelling bigger. "Tell me what you need."

"I need you to fuck me hard, Dev. Like fucking *hard*," I grated out.

He pinched my clit, and I started to come on a long moan. He drove inside me again, still slow, but deep and hard, all while he pinched and rolled my clit between his thumb and forefinger.

"Oh, yeah," he growled. "This is a big one. Let me feel you come on my cock."

My second orgasm rolled right out of the first. He was so heavy, holding me down and right where he wanted me. All I could do was lay there and feel the ripples of pleasure fracturing through my body, spreading sparks of heat from the inside out.

"Yes, fuck yes," he groaned, whipping to a standing position, grabbing my hips, and driving hard and fast.

His relentless pounding felt like heaven, like I needed the roughness to reach full satiation. Finally, one of his hands spread on the middle of my back, and I felt the throbbing pulse of him spilling inside of me.

He grunted, thrusting twice more, before holding himself deep. He growled through his orgasm this time, sounding far more vampire than man.

I lay there a limp mess of limbs, wondering what the hell was going on. I mean, Devraj and I were highly sexual and experimental. But we usually came together with more decorum than that. I knew in that second he walked in the door that if he wasn't fucking me in under a minute, I was going to start biting and clawing to get what I wanted. It seemed he had the same reaction. Or maybe he was just reacting to my wildness.

A hiss and splatter sizzled on the stove. The water was boiling over.

When he pulled out, I sucked in a breath.

He trailed his hand down my spine and hip. "Stay there, love."

He went to the stove and dealt with the pot then returned with a warm rag and pressed it to my pussy. I stood and looked down at myself, while holding the rag between my legs. My camisole half ripped off of me, tights down to my knees, my breasts pink from rubbing against the table.

"I, uh…" Devraj stood there, still panting slightly, staring in confusion at me, completely naked and his cock half-hard again. "I'm not sure what happened there."

"Should I explain it?" I sassed back before pulling up my pants and taking the rag to the laundry room.

He followed me, still naked, still looking baffled. "I'm not usually so beastly. And I just fed from you last night, so I don't understand why I'm reacting this way."

"I felt the same way," I assured him, lifting onto tiptoes to kiss him. "And I didn't mind, if you couldn't tell."

He grinned, hauling me close, his cock pressed against my stomach and harder than it was two seconds ago.

"So dinner first, then I eat you for dessert."

"I have no problem with that."

CHAPTER 4

~DEVRAJ~

RUBEN LAUGHED as he tilted his tumbler of whiskey back and gulped the rest down, his silver skull ring tinkling against the glass as he set it on the coffee table.

"It's true," I told him. "They looked like idiots. Standing there naked beside the pool literally holding their dicks in their hands."

Ruben tossed his head back and laughed harder.

I'd been telling him about one of my last trips before I settled down here in New Orleans. I'd been invited to some warlock's house on the Amalfi Coast. There was a posse of douchebag warlocks being overtly rude to a group of pretty witches there. But then I overheard one talking about using a sleep spell on the blonde to get what he wanted from her later. Basically, what was equivalent to a supernatural roofie.

So I took over and used my skills of glamour to convince them to do a strip tease to Michael Jackson's "Beat It" in front of the pool. I removed the glamour right as they were essentially jacking off their pencil dicks to the hilarity of the girls. Needless to say, they fled the scene, humiliated and confused, much to my own delight.

"I wish I'd been there." Ruben shook his head, still chuckling.

"If you'd been there, you probably would've opted to rip their throats out rather than play a nasty trick on them."

"I'm more in control than that nowadays."

"So you say."

Archie click-clacked to the front door right as I heard soft feminine voices coming up the walk outside. The door opened and Ruben stiffened. I scented Isadora and her sister Jules entering the foyer. Our heightened senses often announced people's arrival before we actually saw them.

"Oh," said Isadora, a little surprised as she entered the living room first, carrying some shopping bags with Jules right behind her. "I didn't know we had company tonight."

Ruben and I stood as they walked in. Isadora kissed me on the cheek before giving Ruben a one-armed hug in greeting, her other laden with bags. She'd gotten to know Ruben a lot more in the past few months, since he was my best friend other than her. Isadora didn't openly show affection for many people, but Ruben had entered that small circle which made me very happy.

What didn't make Ruben or Jules happy was being thrust into each other's presence without fair warning. They both obviously needed time to prepare to mask their emotions and gird their loins against the physical pain of being in one another's presence.

"Hello, Ruben," she said stiffly, lowering the shopping bag from her shoulder to both hands in front of her.

"Jules." He nodded, stuffing his hands into the pockets of his pristine charcoal slacks.

"Well." Jules cleared her throat and walked over to the Christmas tree. "I'll set these here for you, Iz."

"Of course." Isadora joined her, both of them unpacking wrapped presents.

"Looks like the shops are happy you went out today," I said lightly, though it didn't ease the tension ramping up in the room.

"Oh, yeah," laughed Isadora. "They adored us today. We already dumped all of Jules's packages at her house, but she helped me carry mine over."

Ruben stepped closer to the tree, heavy gaze on Jules. As expected.

The sexual tension catapulted to the stratosphere with these two eye-fucking each other while also somehow looking like they hated one another.

"There," said Jules tightly, standing and now avoiding Ruben's gaze. "I better get going then."

"It's late. I'll walk you home," said Ruben.

Jules scoffed. "I'll be fine on my own." She narrowed her pretty eyes. "Or do you not think I can take care of myself?"

"That's not what I meant."

"What did you mean?" she snapped, crossing her arms.

"As much as you like to pretend it, you aren't invincible, Juliana."

Her face flushed pink as she grated out, "I never said I was."

"I'm walking you home whether you want me to or not."

"Fine!" she yelled, sounding very much like a petulant child and then looking like one as she stormed from the room with a hot-tempered vampire overlord in her wake.

After the door slammed, I turned to Isadora, mouth ajar and shook my head. "I think those two may kill each other before they ever realize that a month-long sex romp could easily take that edge off."

Isadora laughed. "I think you're right." Then her gaze turned hot, trailing down my body.

I was still in my dress shirt and black pants, having worked with Ruben all day today and checking on a vampire den on the West Bank that he wanted to be sure was obeying the blood host rules. The closer I walked to Isadora, the harder my dick became.

Christ almighty. My lust burned through my blood like a flaming line of rocket fuel with every step I drew near to her.

She was breathing heavy by the time I reached her, breasts heaving, hands clenching in the long, cream-colored cardigan she wore today.

"Did you have a nice time shopping with your sister?" I swept her long hair back over both shoulders with my hands, pulling it into a ponytail.

"Yes."

"Are you hungry?"

"Not for food."

Wrapping her hair around one fist, I tugged her head back, exposing her long, slender throat. I scraped my sharp canines along her sensitive skin, palming the small of her back and pressing her body to mine. Then I licked back to her ear, lingering over the scraped skin.

"I'm starving, love. For you." I nipped her earlobe.

She flinched as a pearl of blood welled. I sucked her lobe into my mouth, moaning at that tantalizing sweet drop of blood. "Will you feed me, darling?" I asked, noting yet again the harshness of my voice, that same hot hunger scattering my brain cells to the wind.

"Yes," she whispered back, tightening one fist in my hair and rubbing her sweet body against mine.

Archie yipped behind us, prancing around for attention.

"Sorry, little man," I said, scooping Isadora up in my arms. "Daddy needs privacy and the bed for what I have planned." I looked down, her eyes dilated already. "And you better get ready, sweetheart. I'm getting in that ass tonight."

She moaned and nibbled on my neck, sparking the kindling of desire into a conflagration. I could barely get the bedroom door closed before I was ripping her clothes off and falling on her like a lust-crazed animal.

Fortunately for me, my Isadora had claws and teeth of her own. I kissed and sucked every erogenous zone on her body then fucked her mouth, her pussy, and her ass. We didn't stop until we were both replete and exhausted and somehow more in love than ever before.

CHAPTER 5

~ISADORA~

SITTING on the Persian rug next to the Christmas tree in the early morning light, I nibbled on a waffle without syrup and tore little pieces off for Archie.

"Sit. Come on, be a good boy, sit."

Archie danced in a circle three times and wagged his tail, tongue hanging out and orange scruffy fur in his eyes.

"Sit, baby! Be a good boy for Mama."

"Well, you were a good girl for Daddy last night, so I guess I'll oblige." Devraj sauntered in, grinning and wearing boxers only, long hair a mess and scratch marks down his chest.

Oh, hell! And a hickey on his inner thigh. What in the world came over me last night?

He scratched his chest while watching me on the floor with Archie. Giving up on making him obey, I tossed him the last piece of my waffle.

"How are you feeling this morning?" I asked.

The closer he came to me, the bigger the bulge in his boxers grew. The hand on his chest trailed down to grip that bulge. His silvery gaze was on my chest and the gape of my robe. I didn't have anything else on underneath.

"Oh, come on. Are you kidding me? After last night?" My voice rose with disbelief.

"I can't control it," he said.

As soon as he was standing right above me, a wave of hot longing crashed over me. Almost like he'd opened a door and let out a feral beast of lust. I was on my knees, robe slipping off my shoulder, hands at his waistband when it hit me.

I froze.

This wasn't normal. I knew it wasn't, but I'd been letting the lust guide me rather than my brain. When it came to Devraj, that was nothing new.

"Yes, baby," crooned Devraj, hand slipping to my jaw. "Keep going."

I turned to look at the Christmas tree and the ornament right at my eye level.

"I cannot even believe I didn't realize it."

"Realize what?" he asked, turning to look at the tree as if there might be a wild animal in there.

There kind of was. Not an animal, but a wild spell for damn sure.

Even while I was reasoning through the fact that there was a love spell put on that damn ornament, sweltering desire blazed across my skin, my nipples hardening with nothing more than Devraj's hand on my jaw.

"The reason we've been fucking like rabbits," I told him, looking up from where I was still on my knees, "is because Clara put a love spell on that ornament."

His brows puckered, even while he gripped his hard dick over his boxers. "You sure?"

"Positive."

Clara's magical signature is practically undetectable. Because she wields and manipulates emotions and emotions are a natural part of us, it's almost impossible to perceive an Aura's magic at work. And the fact that Dev and I are crazy about each other and each other's bodies, it never occurred to me.

Until just now when I literally felt the spell working, my desire going from zero to sixty the second Dev walked toward me.

"Don't worry," I told him. "I'll take care of it."

He nodded, his expression pleading. "Before that,

can you take care of me, love? I promise I'll reciprocate."

Smiling, I pulled down his boxers and gripped his thick cock, hot as hell and throbbing for release. He sucked in a hiss.

"You always do." Then I took care of my man.

❄

"STOP RIGHT THERE!"

Clara squeaked at my shrill voice in the kitchen of the house, dropping her box of Frosted Flakes.

Funny, I've been slowly thinking of it as *the* house rather than *our* house lately. I suppose Dev's home was slowly but surely becoming mine too.

Clara breathed out a sigh of relief when she saw me then froze when I held out the box with the ornament inside.

"You've got some explaining to do."

She blinked innocently for a moment. Then my sweetest sister got the most devious, devilish look on her face that I have ever seen. It almost made me take a step back.

"Did it work?" she asked, eyes alight with glee.

"Um. Yeah." I shifted from one foot to the other, sensing the soreness between my thighs. And everywhere else. "It worked."

She cackled like the witch she was. "I knew it!"

"But why would you do that to us? It's not like we needed it."

Clara picked up her cereal box and walked to the counter to pour a bowl. "That's because it wasn't meant for you. It was meant for Violet."

"Violet?"

"I figured she'd try to snag it because of the Fred lookalike on the ornament. And she did, but then your man was determined to steal it for you."

She poured the milk and pushed the bowl across the counter then sat on the stool on the other side, spoon in hand.

"Huh. You're right."

Then I realized what Clara's wicked intentions were. "Holy shit. You were trying to get Violet to jump Nico."

"Of course, I was. She is being ridiculously stubborn where Nico is concerned. He's perfect for her, and she keeps him solidly in the friend zone. Time to get things moving."

"So like a good sister, you decided to take things into your own hands."

"Exactly," she said, while crunching a mouthful of cereal.

"What a good sister you are."

"I know," she smiled back at me.

"So, how does this lust potion work exactly?"

I was curious, because it wasn't *on* all the time.

"I prefer calling it a love potion. And it's easy. Once two people who desire one another are in the same vicinity of the potion, it immediately locks onto them and draws them together."

I remembered the way Jules and Ruben got antsy last night standing there in the living room. You could've cut the sexual tension with a butter knife.

"Oh, my God." I laughed so hard, realizing the level of lust that must've been pummeling those two last night while they railed at each other like cats and dogs.

"What?" Clara asked.

"Nothing." I turned and sauntered back toward the back door, ornament in hand.

"Wait! What are you going to do with the ornament?"

"I was thinking of keeping it actually," I told her, because damn it was the most intense aphrodisiac ever. "But I think your intentions were right in the first place."

Clara gave a whoop of excitement as I went to get Devraj so we could take a stroll to Nico and Violet's new shop.

DEVRAJ HELD the door open for me to Empress Ink. The property was attached by a brick and grass enclosed courtyard to Nico's house on a dead-end street. It was a short walk off of Magazine Street, so in a perfect location.

Upon entering, I was drawn to Nico at the top of a ladder in the center of the lobby, Mateo a step behind him, both holding up what looked like a heavy wrought iron chandelier.

Of course, they were both werewolves, so it wouldn't be too heavy for them. Still, their arms were bulging while Nico drilled the fixture into the ceiling.

Livvy was circling them, snapping pics. Violet stood off to the side, tilting her head with hands on hips as she watched. For the first time in a long while, she was letting her natural hair grow out, the tips a light lavender, platinum blond at the top.

"Need help?" asked Devraj.

Nico glanced back. "No, man. We got it. Almost done."

"I've got what I need too," added Livvy, putting the lens camp back on her Nikon. "Gotta run, Vi." She gave me a peck on the cheek as she passed then escaped out the door. Livvy always seemed to be on the run somewhere. She hated being idle.

"Those pics for your Instagram page?" I asked as Livvy left.

"Yeah," said Violet. "Livvy is taking care of all that, thank fuck. Because I have my hands more than full."

"I think my hands are fuller than yours," said Nico from the top of the ladder.

"So funny, wolfie." She rolled her eyes. "What's up, Iz? You want a tour?"

"Well, Devraj and I were just headed to dinner at Gris Gris, but I wanted to bring this by. As a little shop warming gift." I tried not to smile too wide. Violet was perceptive as all hell.

"A present?!" She snatched it out of my hands.

I'd rewrapped it in new paper. She ripped it all off quick as a flash and did a little dance in place when she pulled it out of the box.

"Awww! You're giving me the Fred ornament?"

I laughed. "You seemed pretty excited about it, and I uh, thought you and Nico might like it for your little tree."

Their tree was standing in the corner when you walked into the shop, all lit up and sparsely decorated with ornaments. The shop was still under renovations, but it seemed to be coming along nicely.

"That's the sweetest. Thank you, Iz!" She wrapped me in a one-arm hug then set to unwrapping the plastic wrap.

On that note…

"Well, Dev and I should be going." I laced my fingers

with his hand. He arched an eyebrow at me, but said not a word. "We'll get the full tour when all the remodeling is done."

"That's a good idea," she said.

Mateo and Nico came back down the ladder.

"What do you think?" Nico asked Violet, gesturing toward the chandelier as he took a few steps back toward us.

"Looks fantastic. I knew I picked the right one."

Mateo joined us, scratching the scruff on his chin as he looked at the Christmas tree not the chandelier. His gaze swiveled to the ornament, nostrils flared. "If we're done, I'll be getting home to Evie."

"Thanks, man." Nico clapped him on the back before Mateo hurried out the door.

Nico glanced at the ornament in Violet's hand. "Is that the one you wanted so bad the other night at the party?"

"Yes." She placed it on the tree. "My sister loves me so much, she gave it up for me." Violet gave him a haughty look.

But Nico's gaze had gone molten, rolling with a flash of wolf-green. He clenched his jaw. I could already feel the temperature rising in the room, my body wanting succor from the man at my side.

"We should really get going," I said quickly.

"We'll see you guys at Sunday dinner," added Devraj before he ushered me out the door.

I caught a glimpse of longing in Violet's eyes as she looked over her shoulder at Nico before we were on the sidewalk.

With a breath of cold air outside, we walked along hand-in-hand, laughing a little at the hellstorm of rising sexual tension we left behind us.

"I had no idea you could be so devious." He tugged me closer then wrapped an arm around my waist.

"I can be when necessary."

"Duly noted." He squeezed closer. I wrapped my arm around his as well. "Now let's get my baby fed. We're taking it slow tonight, and I have a full body massage planned first."

"No love spell needed, eh?"

He stopped me in the street and cupped my face carefully with both hands, his palms warming my cheeks.

"Darling. You put that spell on me all on your own. I was bewitched the moment I hit you with my car."

Smiling, I closed my eyes as he swept his lips lightly over mine. "I'm so happy you hit me with your Porsche."

"Oh, now we're being cheeky, are we?"

He reached down and pinched my bottom.

"Hey!" I squirmed away and started walking.

Insulting his Italian luxury car was the quickest way to get a rise out of him.

He caught up and laced his fingers with mine, pressing a kiss to the back of my hand as we strolled along, watching the shoppers hurry here and there. Bright, cheery window displays glowed warmly from each shop, the excitement that only comes with the holidays in the air.

"You know," he offered, "we could get Gris Gris to go?"

"And bring it home instead."

He slid that melty smile my way. "How about a little picnic on the rug in front of the fire?"

I smiled up at him, shivering at a particularly lovely memory on that rug when we first started dating.

I suddenly realized I'd thought of his house as *my home* for the first time, rather than my parents' house where they'd raised us. The one I'd lived in all my life until a few months ago

I suppose that was natural though. Once your heart found its match, home was wherever they were. I sighed happily, hoping my sisters would find their own soulmates as well. Evie and I had found ours, and I wanted everyone to know the bliss of deep and binding true love. At the very least, I can say I did my part in giving Violet a shove in the right direction.

"Do you think I did the right thing in giving that

ornament to Violet and Nico?" I asked, unsure of myself now.

"Without a doubt," said Devraj. "Nico has been a patient man. Maybe a little unbridled lust will kick your sister's butt into gear."

"Hopefully." I laughed. "So you think Nico still wants her? He's been around for a while with Violet not budging an inch."

He chuckled, his breath coming out in white puffs as the temperature dropped. "I know wholeheartedly that he does."

"How's that?"

He gazed down at me, keeping me close to his side as we walked along then he whispered softly, "Because he looks at her the way I look at you." Then he gave me a swift kiss. "Trust me, we did a service for love tonight. And now, all I want to do is service you."

"You sure you aren't having lingering effects of that love spell?" I teased.

"Not at all. This is all me, my love."

"Then let's get home."

JINGLE BELL JOCK

Timeline: Takes place during* **Witches Get Stitches.

CHAPTER 1

~CHARLIE~

FALLING in love with your best friend is not wise. I highly recommend that you do not do this.

It was hitting home harder than usual tonight, New Year's Eve, because here I was, currently standing across the party watching JJ flirt with some guy in a cable-knit sweater, corduroy pants, and an overly gelled hairstyle. Despite his failed fashion choices, he was hot.

JJ also happened to be wearing that rare smile he often wore when he was genuinely engaged with someone.

I have been one of the few people fortunate enough

to have that smile bestowed upon them. But not tonight. Cable-knit sweater guy was getting it.

And that's when I realized I'd had enough. This sickening nausea I experienced every time I thought of JJ with another man was slowly destroying me inside.

I swear, that song "Killing Me Softly" could be my daily mantra at this point.

But it was a new year, and I was determined to turn over a new leaf. To stop pining after my best friend who would never see me as anything more than that and move on.

"Hi. It's Charlie, right?"

Well, *hello*. Were the dating gods listening tonight?

"Yes, hi?"

I'm sure I looked puzzled, trying to figure out if we'd met before. But I didn't want to give him that cheesy pick-up line, *have we met somewhere before?*

"Thomas Baylor." He shook my hand. The one not holding the import beer.

He was taller than me, which I liked. Nice physique and seriously kind eyes. Deep brown, heavily lashed, and intelligent.

He glanced away nervously before saying, "Before you ask, no, we haven't met. I just asked Isaac who you were."

Isaac was the host of the party. I glanced toward the

kitchen where Isaac was surrounded by a throng. He winked in my direction.

"Nice to meet you," I turned back to him, giving him my full attention. "How do you know Isaac?"

"Work."

"You work at the gallery?"

"Not exactly. I help with installations for the larger exhibits. It's a rather unusual company, actually. We basically help with the staging of large estates going on sale, art galleries, and stuff like that.

He had an attractive, mellow voice. He was nice and appeared fit as well beneath that long-sleeved, button-down.

"That sounds like interesting work."

"Sometimes," he flashed me a wide smile. "What do you do?"

I gestured toward the balcony which faced the direction of Canal Street. "I'm the Event Manager for the Hilton."

His eyes widened. "Now that sounds far more interesting than my work."

A loud boom and pop outside drew everyone's attention to the windows.

"Looks like some early fireworks," said Thomas. "Want to go watch?"

His sweet smile had already lured me in. He was

younger than me, maybe mid-twenties, but I liked him. And more to the point, *he* seemed to like *me*.

"Sure. Let's grab another beer."

We stopped at the bar in the kitchen and grabbed two more Heinekens. I walked ahead of Thomas and pulled open the balcony door. He braced a hand at the small of my back when a rowdy chick and another guy came barreling back inside, nearly knocking us over. I have to say, Thomas's protective gesture gave me a nice, melty feeling.

And quickly following that sensation was the feeling of betrayal. I wasn't betraying JJ. We weren't together. And yet, that didn't make a damn bit of difference to my sad, besotted heart.

Still, this was a good step. I hadn't dated anyone in a while. And my longing for JJ had reached a ridiculous level where I needed to do something.

Thomas was the something. I mean, not that I was going to *do* him tonight or anything. I needed to get to know him first. I was quite the flirt, but I was very discriminating about the men I welcomed into my bed. I wasn't a one-night stand kind of guy. I didn't begrudge others for it, but believe it or not, I was somewhat shy and reticent when it came to sex.

Don't get me wrong. I enjoyed it. *Immensely*. But I had to have some level of trust with a man before we went there.

We took up a free spot at the balcony and watched some of the fireworks shooting off on the West Bank. There would be even bigger ones in about an hour at midnight.

"So, uh," Thomas stammered, both his forearms braced on the balcony railing, beer still in hand, "I know I'm being forward and all, but are you dating anyone?"

He ducked his head shyly before returning his gaze back to me.

"No." Unfortunately. "I'm not."

"Good," he gave a nervous laugh and sipped his beer. "I didn't want to make a fool of myself if you were here with someone."

He was direct but sweet, which I found refreshingly charming.

"I'm here with JJ. He's my best friend." And that was all. "So, you're in the clear. Please continue flirting."

He belted out a laugh, flashing those pearly whites, and I found I was surprisingly distracted from the pity party I'd been throwing myself all night.

Thomas then entertained me with some funny work stories. For example, the time he installed the abstract sculpture wrong and the artist lost her damn mind when as he put it, *you couldn't tell the head from the ass on that weird sculpture.*

I then shared some horror stories of my own with

corporate clients. Like the one who nearly blew a blood vessel because his Evian water wasn't exactly 65 degrees as requested.

He laughed that infectious laugh again. "People are such assholes."

"They are." I agreed, finishing my beer and putting it on the table behind me where he'd set his empty bottle too. "Some people just like to complain because it makes them feel important."

"Why is that? I mean, couldn't they feel just as important by getting attention for being nice."

Wow. Thomas had a good heart. I could feel it in the way he spoke about others, even the hard-to-please artists he had to deal with. He was respectful and kind and definitely someone I could develop feelings for.

The big fireworks near the French Quarter started popping, shimmering on the Mississippi River like broken glass. Sparkles of fluorescent pinks, purples, and greens glittered in the night sky. We watched in silence, his arm touching mine on the railing. I had a nice buzz, and the cool breeze coming off the river in the near distance put me in a dreamy sort of mood.

Then they started counting down to midnight inside. And I could feel Thomas staring at me.

"I really like you," he practically whispered.

Turning to him, I realized we'd somehow moved closer where our faces were inches apart.

"I like you, too," I told him honestly.

Those brown eyes watched me closely as if trying to determine something. I was fairly sure I knew what it was. When everyone erupted inside, screaming *Happy New Year,* he leaned closer and brushed his lips to mine. Tentative and soft. When I opened my mouth for him, he angled his head and swept his tongue inside on a little moan.

I cupped his jaw and kissed him back, enjoying this sensation of being desired.

Don't get me wrong. I wasn't hard-up for dates if I wanted them. But I wanted more than a hook-up. What I truly wanted, I couldn't have, because he was currently inside probably making out with Cable-knit Guy.

But Thomas was the first man I'd had any sort of connection with who made me consider hanging up my obsession/lost cause with JJ. Even in this short time of knowing him, I felt something tender with possibility blooming between us.

He combed his fingers through my hair and along the back of my nape, holding me closer and kissing me deeper. I rode the heady sensation of desire with him, kissing the fuck out of his sweet mouth.

Then I wondered—not for the first or second time—what it would feel like to kiss JJ. I doubt it would be soft like this. I moaned at the thought of JJ kissing me, which had Thomas gripping my hip and pulling me closer. I broke the kiss, feeling like I was doing something wrong.

"I'm sorry. I didn't mean to, uh, get carried away." Thomas dropped his hand from my neck but kept the other on my hip.

I heard the door closing to the balcony. When I glanced over my shoulder, I caught the broad back of my best friend returning to the party.

My heart squeezed at the thought of him seeing me kissing Thomas. But then I remembered that we were just friends. And that all my wishful thinking that he'd be jealous and would finally stake his claim on me was ridiculous fantasy.

"I would love to take you out," Thomas broke into my musing. "Could I get your number?"

My attention back on those warm brown eyes, I realized I had to let go for good.

"Yes. You certainly can."

CHAPTER 2

~JJ~

THE FIRST THING I remembered when I sat up in bed, head spinning with the worst fucking hangover in my adult history, was a vision of that twat-waffle Thomas kissing Charlie.

Okay, maybe he wasn't a twat-waffle. But the more Isaac sang his praises, the more I hated the kid. As soon as I saw him with his hands and mouth all over Charlie on the balcony, I'd spent the next hour interrogating Isaac while shooting tequila.

It was my job as Charlie's best friend to make sure he wasn't hooking up with another douchebag. Because Charlie was good at not being very selective with the guys he dated. I'd had to scare off one or two who'd become obsessed with him.

The thing was about Charlie was that he was so magnetic that the men he dated always fell in love with him on the first date. Then if Charlie wasn't interested anymore, they sometimes didn't take the hint very easily. He was lucky he had a friend like me looking out for him.

So yeah, I interrogated the fuck out of Isaac about this guy Thomas sticking his tongue down Charlie's throat.

Maybe I could've held back on my snide comments when Charlie practically scraped me off the bar to drive me home later. I think I said something about not wanting to interrupt him if he was getting his New Year lay.

Fuck. What an asshole I am.

I'd never reacted like that before when he was dating other guys. Not until they became a problem for Charlie and he needed my help getting them to back off. But for some reason last night, it felt like a kick in the guts. And the balls. And to be honest, the heart.

I had a visceral reaction to walking out onto the balcony where I planned to give my best friend a bear hug and wish him Happy New Year, only to find some young toddler groping him and kissing the fuck out of him.

Nausea swelled in my stomach again.

I hurried to the bathroom but fortunately, or maybe unfortunately, nothing came back up. I looked like total shit, and I was working the day shift. Who was I kidding? I worked every day, though I'd started training Finny on the bar.

I was the sole bartender for The Cauldron though Belinda, Evie, and Violet could all make the drinks on the slow days. That's when I typically didn't go in until the afternoon. But it was New Year's Day and Jules would have some fancy specials for all the hungover people of the lower Garden District looking for a good, greasy meal. I was one of them.

Groaning at the apology I needed to make to Charlie, I showered, trimmed my beard, and dressed in jeans and a Henley.

"Morning, Miko."

My calico cat meowed, standing on the sofa back. She walked alongside me through the living room, needing her good morning stroke. After a little petting, I headed to the laundry room and filled her bowl.

Downing a bottle of water and some Advil, I grabbed my phone, plugged into the charger on the kitchen counter by the back door then remembered how Charlie had wrestled it away from me to plug it in last night before I passed out in my bedroom.

I winced at the memory of how mean I was to him.

I let Miko outside before I shut the door. She preferred spending her days lounging on my porch, torturing lizards, pretending she was queen of the jungle, till I got home.

"Be a good girl."

She blinked heavily at me, telling me she probably wouldn't be. There was a good chance I'd find some poor dead creature on my doorstep as a gift when I got home just for daring to tell her what to do.

Hopping into my Jeep, I made the short drive to The Cauldron. Some days I walked to work for the exercise. But today, I'd be lucky if I could stand up for the whole shift. As soon as I parked along the street, I made my way through the back alley and into the kitchen since the front door wasn't open yet.

One of the line cooks Sam was prepping onions. That turned my stomach. But Jules was already stirring something that smelled divine.

"What are the specials today?" I asked, coming up behind her to peer in the pot.

I was the only one she allowed to do this without getting their head bitten off.

"Duck and sausage gumbo. And we'll have the traditional New Year's Day ham, smothered cabbage with sausage, and black-eyed peas."

"Could I get a bowl of that gumbo?"

She took a good look at me, obviously seeing how

pathetic I felt. I wished it was only because of the alcohol. But my emotions were running riot inside me right now.

"Grab some French bread. You look like you need something to soak up the alcohol in your system."

I nodded without comment and pulled a fresh loaf off the shelf. Jules had a deal with Queen of Tarts across the street and often bought their sweets and breads for the restaurant.

Jules set down a bowl of gumbo, the dark roux steaming, and a side of potato salad. "Was it a fun night or one of those you'd rather forget?"

"A little of both."

"JJ," she said teasingly, "I can't imagine you doing anything out of order."

"Am I that boring?"

She leaned her hip against the stainless-steel counter, arms crossed, while I wolfed down the gumbo and bread, already feeling light-years better.

"You're the reliable one. What? Charlie let you get out of hand last night?"

Charlie was the reason I got totally bent last night. But I couldn't tell her that.

"Jules, do you want this thin sliced?" Sam called from where he was pulling one of several honey hams out of the roaster.

"I'll do that."

She left me to my own miserable thoughts, thankfully. I dunked the last piece of bread into the gumbo and finished off the rest. After taking the dishes to the back and washing them, I headed back to the bar with a fresh rack of tumbler glasses.

Evie was bustling around, wiping down some of the tables that hadn't been cleaned well enough last night. She was a hustler, and I loved that about her.

"Hey, woman," I called over as I stacked the glasses for the day. "Haven't seen you in a little while. Your man keeping you busy?"

I was protective of the Savoie sisters, treating them as if they were my own. And while I had my doubts about that werewolf Mateo, at first, I wholeheartedly approved of the relationship now. He was devoted to her and treated her like a queen. She deserved it. All the Savoie women did.

"Heyyy!" She meandered through the two-tops and plopped herself on a barstool across from me. "I took a few days off because I had a little stomach flu. Really wore me out. I was so tired." She smiled brightly. "But I feel better now. How about you? How was New Year's Eve? You and Charlie go out?"

I nodded, wiping the glasses before I stacked them. "Yeah. Went to a friend's party."

"Uh oh. That doesn't sound good."

"What do you mean?" I made sure to keep a

perfectly even tone so she wouldn't detect anything. But again, she was a witch.

"Did you and Charlie get in a fight?"

"Why would you ask that? Charlie and I don't fight."

"Exactly. But I'm getting sad vibes, like regret and shame and stuff coming off you. What did you do?"

"Christ, Evie. I thought Clara was the one who could read emotions. Since when do you—?"

"Did someone call me?" Clara appeared out of thin air; I swear.

I jumped. "When did you get here?"

"Clara, come here and tell me what JJ did because he won't say." Then Evie proceeded to relay our brief conversation from ten seconds ago.

I leaned against the counter, strangling my dish towel in one hand, trying not to glare at Clara while she observed my aura carefully.

Then she knocked my knees out from under me. "You hurt Charlie's feelings."

"JJ!" Evie screamed. "How could you do such a thing? He's your best friend!"

Meanwhile, I stood, mouth agape, because how the hell did Clara guess that?

"How do you do that?"

Clara looked at me with a pitying expression, "It's what I do," she said cryptically. "What happened? Did y'all fight about something?"

"No," I growled, moving some imports to the glass-encased freezer to get cool for the lunch rush. I heaved a sigh. "I made fun of this guy he was hooking up with."

"Why?" asked Evie. "You didn't like him?"

I shrugged. "He just irritated me. I was looking forward to spending some time with my best friend, but this teenager hogged him the whole damn night."

"Charlie was making out with a teenager?!" Evie's eyes nearly bugged out of her head.

"Not really a teenager." I frowned. "But he was too damn young for Charlie who needs someone more mature. Not some young stud who's just sowing his oats."

"Some people mature early," added Clara thoughtfully. "He could be one of those old souls. He could be Charlie's soulmate, as a matter of fact."

I whirled in anger, catching Clara smiling at Evie before she wiped it away, looking back at me. "You didn't see him. He looked like…"

"Like?" Evie waved her hand in a circular motion for me to continue.

"Like not Charlie's type." I turned back to the cooler, clanking bottles a little too hard.

"I see," said Evie, "Well, why don't we just ask him about this new guy?"

My stomach dropped out from under me as I heard

Evie go to the front door and unlock it. When I turned, she was giving Charlie a hug.

He looked really good. Not like dogshit, like me. Fresh, his blond hair perfectly styled, casual work attire, his usual tilted smile that made me want to lean in and kiss him.

WHAT?!

Where the fuck had that thought come from?

I didn't want to kiss Charlie!

Wait. I wanted to kiss Charlie?

Gulping hard against this new discovery, I watched him chit-chat with Evie as he walked over. It was when his gaze hit mine, his smile slipping, that my heartrate quickened into something akin to panic.

He was upset with me. And that tripled the weight of my regret from last night.

But he took up his regular stool at the end closest to the kitchen and replied to Evie, "Just my regular, thanks."

"No problem." She dropped a place setting next to him and gave him a smile, then narrowed her eyes at me with a mean face when he turned away.

Damn, I was on everyone's shit list, it appeared. Time to make amends.

"Hey." I wiped my hands with my dish rag, needing something to do with them so I wouldn't pull my hair out in frustration. "Listen, uh—"

He had his hands clasped loosely on the bar-top and gave me that serene look he always wore. To say it was unnerving was an understatement. I could feel how upset he was without him saying a word.

"About last night," I continued, clearing my throat, "I'm really sorry for being a total ass."

He smiled, avoiding my gaze. "It's okay."

"No, seriously. I shouldn't have been like that with you. If you, you know, like Thomas or whatever, I'll keep my mouth shut."

He angled his head, the light from the window shooting across his hair, making it glow like a fucking halo. I knew he was no angel, but everything about him today seemed...divine. And I felt like the devil cast out of his circle. My stomach twisted into knots.

"What is it you don't like about him?"

Grinding my teeth, I turned to the bar behind me and made him an iced tea, knowing he was heading back to work after lunch. The hotel didn't keep most holidays, even those in administration like him were required to be at work on days like today. But he always took a long lunch and worked later to make up the difference. I was glad he decided to stop in today to see me, especially since I didn't deserve it. He took lunch here a couple days a week, but I definitely didn't expect him today.

I set the iced tea on a napkin in front of him and slid

a straw across the counter. "Isn't he a little young for you?" I asked quietly.

Charlie's brow puckered into a frown and he smiled at the same time. "He's twenty-five."

"Exactly. And you're thirty-one."

"And you're thirty-seven, the same number of years apart. And yet we're still best friends," he snapped. Then he tilted his head questioningly. "Aren't we?"

"*Yes*. Of course, we are. Why would you ask something like that?"

"I don't know. Last night, you seemed really upset with me."

"I was drunk last night and was out of my head. I'm sorry. I don't even remember half of what I said"—which was true and for which I was grateful, but what I did remember made me wince—"but I apologize for all of it."

He nodded and sipped his tea, which drew my attention to his lips wrapped around the straw. When he swiped his tongue across his bottom lip, my cock twitched. I flinched.

"Are you okay?" He seemed genuinely concerned about me.

He probably should be. Because I wasn't okay. Not even fucking close. I was lusting after my best friend and imagining things I wanted him to do with his perfect, beautiful, fucking mouth.

Needing to get back on the offensive before I lost my damn mind, I said, "You may be only six years apart, but mid-twenties is totally different than being in your thirties."

"How so?"

I scoffed. "Come on, Charlie. Remember what it was like in your twenties? Trying on every new guy for a good ride?"

He frowned at that. "You might have. But I've kept to monogamous relationships, not bed-hopping. Even in my twenties."

True. I was pretty much a manwhore and enjoyed the hell out of my wilder days. It had lost its luster when I hit my thirties. But Charlie was never like me in that regard.

"But still," I continued, "you don't always make the best decisions in dating."

"That's why it's called *dating*, Jeremy. I'm not marrying him." Then he mumbled, "Yet."

He might as well have picked up the butter knife sitting next to him and cut my heart out. And the fact that he was using my full name told me he hadn't quite forgiven me yet.

"Yeah," I agreed, hoping I didn't sound as utterly gutted as I felt. "You're right."

Then he carried on the conversation about Isaac's

antics last night, while I wiped down the counter and pretended I wasn't dying inside.

All I could think as I watched him eat his lunch and entertain me with the events from last night that I couldn't remember was that it's a rather unnerving—and somewhat devastating—feeling when you discover that you want to fuck your best friend.

CHAPTER 3

~CHARLIE~

"SHUT IT. AND GOODNIGHT."

Violet swished by me, mumbled something to Clara sitting next to me at the bar then fled out of The Cauldron like a demon was after her.

Maybe I was a bit too pushy with her tonight. I glanced back at Nico, her sexy AF werewolf business partner, as he crooned into the microphone on the stage. He had a harsh look about him tonight. I wondered what Violet had said to him.

All I'd told her was that it was time she stopped beating around the goddamn bush and jumped that hunk of man. He wanted her. I knew it. Everyone knew it. And she wanted him. But Violet was stubborn as fuck.

Which reminded me that she told me I was stubborn too. Not only that. She'd revealed something I didn't know. That she'd done a reading about me and JJ. Violet was a Seer, the kind of witch who could see visions and make predictions. And she'd told me flat-out that the two of us belonged together.

I watched JJ talking to a customer in his friendly way. He was so handsome my lungs seized up, and I couldn't catch my breath. My chest tightened if I stared too long. His hazel eyes snagged on me for a few seconds, the connection intimate in a way I hadn't felt before, then he returned his attention to the customer.

"You okay?" Clara asked.

She'd been entertaining the new tattoo artist Lindsey, since Violet had bailed on hosting her first night in town. Lindsey had slipped off to the bathroom.

"Yeah, why?" I removed the cocktail straw from my Poison Apple Sangria. JJ always made the best sangrias.

"Your aura is telling me that you're confused and sad about something."

"My aura talks to you?"

Clara's blue eyes glittered brightly under the bar lights. "Not with words, but yes. My magic speaks to me. I'm pretty sure I know what all this is about."

"Really?"

"Ninety-two percent sure."

Only Clara would have such a high and yet strangely not high enough percentage of surety about something.

I smiled. "I'd love to find out if you're in the eight percent of wrong or not."

She blinked twice, her expression becoming far graver than I was accustomed to seeing on Clara. She was the worry-free Savoie sister, always joyful and serene. But right here before me in a crowded, loud bar, her eyes welled with tears.

"Charlie," she whispered. "You're confused because you're with the wrong man. You're sad because your heart knows it."

The air vacated my lungs. My pulse rocketed with a jolt of adrenaline.

"What?" I asked, my voice so low it was little more than a puff of air.

She placed her hand on mine but didn't try to spell me as she had before when she wanted to me happy. Instead, she blinked again and a tear trekked down her rosy cheek. My chest ached at the sincere sorrow pouring off her.

"You belong with JJ." She gave me a sweet smile. "And he belongs with you."

"But he—"

She squeezed my arm and shook her head. "No buts,

Charlie. It's the truth. And you need to face it if you ever want to fill that aching hole inside of you."

"It's not me you should be talking to," I told her, a little shocked that I was even having this conversation. Clara and I had never talked like this before.

She cupped my face and patted me like I was a child. "Be brave when the time comes." Then she popped off the stool and met Lindsey closer to the stage where Nico was still singing some ridiculously sexy ballad.

I stared into my sangria, wondering where the hell that had come from when I heard JJ say, "So you going to Isaac's new exhibit this weekend? He's showcasing one of those surrealist artists you like."

Wiping away all the emotion trying to bleed out of my pores, I took a sip of my drink and tried to sound normal. "Uh, I hadn't thought about it."

JJ wore that same tight expression he'd been wearing around me the past few weeks. He didn't like Thomas, so he'd been avoiding me a lot.

"Why don't you come with me?" he asked, those hazel eyes intense and focused.

I guess he wasn't avoiding me anymore.

"Unless you're already going out with Thomas," he added, his jaw tightening.

"Not this weekend."

"Why not?"

"He's got a family thing."

He stared at me a few seconds, both of his palms on the bar which flexed his arms distractingly. "You aren't going with him?"

Stirring my ice cubes around with a cocktail straw, I shook my head. "Not sure I want to meet the family yet. Though he'd asked me to go."

Typically, JJ would pepper me with a hundred questions about whatever guy I was dating and tell me what I should be doing and how and why. But not this time. Whatever bothered him about Thomas had shut him up. Maybe it was because of what happened on New Year's Eve.

He had hurt my feelings, no matter that he had remembered saying those things or not. He'd scolded me brutally about *fucking my new toy* and ringing in the New Year with *a good blow job.* None of which had happened.

Instead, I had the glorious privilege of hauling his drunk ass home, which was very difficult because he had at least sixty pounds on me.

Once I'd stumbled with him into his house and to his bed, where he flopped on his back, I took off his socks and shoes. Before he passed out, he managed to pull off his shirt before falling unconscious again.

Seeing all that magnificent, muscular skin was agonizing. A torture I had to squeeze my eyes shut tight and try to forget.

Thomas. I remembered how sweet and kind he'd been to me that night. How nice his kiss had been. How I'd agreed to go out with him.

So, without further ado, I walked back through JJ's house, gave Miko some water since her bowl was empty, petted her, and locked the door as I left.

"You want to go?" he asked, raising his brow. "With me?"

Interesting. I rarely heard that particular tone of uncertainty on JJ. He was a force of self-confidence. Unwavering in everything he did. But for some reason, he seemed...nervous?

"Sure. I can meet you at—"

"No, no. I'll pick you up. Say six? We can grab some dinner before."

Weird. We typically just meet out somewhere. But JJ had that stern, determined look back on his face. The one he wore when he was going to get what he wanted.

"Fine," I told him, confused at the expression of relief washing away the tightness of his features.

"Good." He nodded before reaching over and squeezing my hand then walking away.

I tried not to read into that. But it was weird. Between Violet's confession that she'd done a reading on us, and Clara's similar declaration that JJ and I belonged together, I was getting all of these signs shooting me toward that same conclusion.

It was like that slow climb up the big hill of a roller coaster. *Tick, tick, tick.* I could feel the car rising toward some inevitable weight-defying, stomach-twisting drop on the other side. What I didn't know was whether the ride would make me laugh or cry.

I wasn't a huge fan of rollercoasters and thrill rides because I wasn't a fan of being surprised. The problem was I could feel the fall coming, whether I wanted to get on or not.

CHAPTER 4

~JJ~

Meow.

"Almost there, my girl," I told Miko in her carrier as I strode up Devraj's walkway then knocked on the door.

Within a minute, Isadora swung it open. She wore one of her Boho skirts and a cream-colored tank with a sage green cardigan. Her long, blond hair was braided over one shoulder. "Hi! You're early."

"Am I?" I glanced down at my watch.

"Yeah," she laughed. "Like almost an hour."

"Oh." I fidgeted, biting my bottom lip.

"Y'all come on in."

I followed her into the living room and glanced around.

"Don't worry. Archie's in the backyard." She took the carrier from me and peered inside, speaking softer. "Don't worry, Miko. He won't get you."

She meowed in a sweet kitty voice not the demanding one I typically got. Miko loved Isadora. But she hated Archie.

"Come on, girl." She sat down on the white fur rug in front of the fireplace, which crackled with a nice fire. She unlatched the carrier and opened the door then scooped her out. "It's okay, Miko," she said in that melodic voice that raised the hairs on my arms.

Though I wasn't magic obviously, I could usually sense when one of the sisters was using it. Isadora gave off this radiant wave whenever she gave Miko her treatments. Miko wasn't very old, but she'd had a bout of leukemia a year ago. This is almost always terminal for cats, but Isadora gave Miko regular healing treatments to keep her healthy and spry. Who would rid my neighborhood of lizards, otherwise?

Isadora simply petted her and cooed sweetly to Miko who had curled up in her lap and purred, obviously enjoying her treatment.

"So what's on your mind?"

I chuckled. "That obvious?"

"Doesn't take a witch to notice how fidgety and anxious you are."

Clearing my throat, I rubbed my sweaty palms on my jeans. "Guess not."

Isadora continued her kitty massage, one hand overlapping the other. The fire popped. I tried to get my nerve up to talk to her. But in true Isadora fashion, she didn't rush me or question me or even look at me. She kept quiet, focusing on Miko, and waited for me to get on with it.

I finally did, blurting, "I'm in love with Charlie."

Her hands paused for a fraction of a second then she continued petting Miko, not looking up at me. Still, I saw a smile spread across her face.

Finally, she asked, "And what are you going to do about it?"

Heart hammering in my throat, I said, "I'm taking him out on a date."

"That's a start."

"But he doesn't know it's a date."

"How is that possible?"

"Well, he thinks we're just hanging out as friends. But I—" I gulped, trying to figure out where all the saliva in my mouth went— "I intend this to be our first date."

"Don't you think you should inform him of this?"

"No."

"Why not?"

"Because he's dating someone else."

Isadora stopped petting Miko, keeping her hands on her and radiating that electric energy as she finally met my gaze, her green eyes sparking brightly with magic.

"JJ. That's a little underhanded. You can't steal him from another man."

"That's just it," I explained, leaning forward in my chair, "we're meant to be together. I know it. I think I've known it for a long time, but I couldn't get enough courage up to tell him or take the chance. I couldn't risk him..."

I stared into the fire, trying to find the words.

"You're afraid he'll reject you."

Nodding, I combed my fingers through my hair, lacing them at the back of my neck, elbows on my knees, waiting for her to tell me the worst. That I was likely to be rejected. That I'd likely lost my chance.

"JJ," she finally said softly in that same silvery voice she used on Miko. "If Charlie is meant for you"—I shot my head up, knowing I wore an expression of terror at what she was going to say next— "and I believe that he is, then you need to be honest with him."

"Wait. You believe that we are meant to be together."

She laughed, brightening her angelic looking face. "Everyone seems to know that but you two."

"Do you think he knows it?"

She shrugged. "The point is. You can't take him on a date and expect him to react to you as a *date* would when he's seeing someone else. He's going to think this is a friend thing. Not a more-than-friends thing."

"But I thought I'd ease him into it slowly, you know? Like take him out and maybe put some feelers out?"

"Explain to me what you mean by feelers." She smirked at me, which was an unusual expression for Isadora. She wasn't the snarky sister. Violet and Livvy were.

"I'll just, you know, maybe see how things are going with Thomas and if that's really going anywhere. Maybe suggest that Thomas isn't the right guy for him."

"Wrong." She shook her head. "Don't do that."

"You're right." I winced. "That would be a douchey thing to do."

"If you take him out, just be yourself and don't warn him against the guy you're trying to steal him from. Instead, tell him how you feel. And see if he returns those feelings."

"Tell him I'm in love with him? Because holy fuck, Iz, you're the first person I've admitted it to besides myself, and I can barely say it without wanting to throw up."

Her smile reminded me of one Clara might give me, one of understanding and compassion. I stood and paced behind the coffee table, watching Archie chasing something I couldn't see in the back yard.

"JJ, listen to me. If what you're telling me is true, that you truly feel this way about Charlie."

"I do."

"Then you *have* to tell him. The universe is bashing you over the head. That's why it's pouring out of you and you look like you're about to run away right out the door."

"My heart is about to pound out of my chest." I clutched at it, trying to steady the booming beneath my skin. "What do I do if he rejects me?"

She gave me that sympathetic look again. "That's something you'll have to face."

"I can't lose him as my best friend. It would kill me, Iz."

"You won't. I know that for sure."

"You do? You can see it like Violet can?"

She smiled. "Not like Violet, no. But I am positive he could handle this bump."

The problem was, I didn't think I could. I didn't want to lose him altogether, but I also felt this incredible need to tell him.

Isadora put a sleeping Miko back in her carrier and softly clicked it locked before rising and handing her over.

"Thank you, Isadora." I leaned forward and gave her a one-armed hug. "I think I needed this push."

Come hell or high water, I was going to find a way to tell him. She rose up on her toes and kissed my cheek, shocking me. Isadora wasn't as openly affectionate as her sisters, but I suppose she knew I needed it.

"It's going to be okay. Trust me."

I gave a her a stiff nod, trying to let her words sink in and headed toward the door. Before I made it, I heard, "Hey, JJ. Hold up."

It was Devraj coming from the hallway. He flashed a sheepish grin.

"Yeah?"

"I, uh, wanted to give you something. Sorry, but I overheard and thought this might come in handy." He handed me a small plastic bag. "If things go well."

"Thanks, man." I took the bag, wondering what the hell was inside it.

He gave me a clap on the shoulder. "Good luck."

Once I'd gotten Miko safely stowed in the backseat of the Jeep, I opened the bag to find a bottle of oil. It advertised *self-heating for maximum pleasure*.

Blood rushed to my face and my dick at the same time. I hadn't let my thoughts stray too far with Charlie. I mean, I had but I'd been consciously trying not to go *there* just in case this all fell apart.

I wasn't sure whether to thank Devraj or damn him. Because this could all go to hell in a handbasket really fast.

Without thinking too hard about it, I tossed the oil back in the bag and set it next to the carrier then hopped in the driver's seat.

Meow.

"I know, baby girl. I know."

First things first. I had to prepare for this date that Charlie didn't know was a date.

CHAPTER 5

~JJ~

"DAMMIT! I need the silver one. Where is it, Miko?"

She didn't answer me from her perch on the back of the couch, twitching her tail as I rushed through the kitchen to the laundry room. There was the thin tie, hanging on the rack above the washer.

I looped it around the collar of my black button-down and tied it in front of the mirror on the living room wall. I'd spent far more time than normal on my grooming, which had now put me behind. I didn't want to be late for my first date with Charlie.

"Not that he even knows it's a date," I muttered to my reflection.

Meow.

"None of your sass," I told Miko, tightening the knot in the tie.

Grabbing my wallet, keys, and the envelope, I left the lamp on for Miko then took off. Charlie lived in nice, but overpriced, apartment building on St. Charles Avenue. In my opinion anyway. The Georgian was in a posh area with the streetcar line running right out front. It was an older but remodeled red brick building with ivy crawling up the sides and surrounded by old oak trees. It was beautiful, but he didn't even have a thousand square feet.

Honestly, he'd be better off living with me. I had an extra bedroom in my house he could rent from me if he liked. I'd even mentioned it before, but he'd said no without giving me a reason. He was neater than me, but I wasn't a slob either.

I imagined for the briefest of seconds what it would be like having him living in my house, walking into the kitchen shirtless in the morning to grab some coffee or breakfast. Then I instantly wiped that vision away. Having an obvious hard-on when I picked him up might not be the best way to start off the night.

I took the elevator to his floor and exhaled a heavy breath before knocking on the door. After a few seconds, he opened the door.

God above, he looked amazing.

He always did, but when he dressed for these events, wearing tailored slacks and a white starched shirt that contrasted with his tan skin. He made my mouth water. He stood there, staring at me with the most confused expression on his beautiful face.

"You didn't have to come up. You could've just texted like usual."

It was true. I didn't normally come up to the apartment when we rode together somewhere, but this was different. Tonight was different. We were different. I hoped.

"I wanted to, uh, see your new furniture. Didn't you get new furniture?"

He widened the door and looked back into the small living space. "You were with me when I picked out the coffee table."

I leaned through the open door to take a look at it, pretending to care what the hell his coffee table looked like. And that was a big fucking mistake. I inhaled a big whiff of him. Whatever expensive cologne he wore, a subtle scent, mixed with his own warm flavor had my brain misfiring.

"Yep. Looks good. Let's get going."

He laughed and followed me out, locking it on the way out. In the elevator, I kept my hands in my pockets and tried not to notice him in the reflection. Or the fact that he glanced at me a couple times, probably wondering what the hell was wrong with me.

I almost pulled what I'd brought for him from my pocket, but I needed to calm down and not come across as some kind of manic freak. He knew my behavior was off. So did I. But could you blame me?!

Tonight was the night. I had to dig up the courage to tell Charlie what I'd realized, how I felt. But I couldn't just blurt it out. I had to calm the hell down before I turned and screamed it in his face like a lunatic.

"Where'd you want to pick up some dinner?" he asked as we headed out of the building to my Jeep.

I unlocked the doors with my key fob and reached out to open his door before quickly withdrawing it, because that might be too obvious. I never opened his car door for him. I needed to warm him up to the idea.

He glanced at me, his brow pinched together in confusion again. I rounded the front of the Jeep and hopped in.

"I wanted to take you to Gris Gris," I told him as I pulled out and swiveled back toward Magazine Street.

"Oh." He sounded surprised. Maybe disappointed?

"You don't want to go there?"

"No, it's not that." He glanced my way and shifted in his seat. "I just figured we'd pick up something quick and easy like at Tracey's Pub. Didn't realize we were doing fancy dinner tonight."

Exhaling a slow, steady breath, I replied, "I know you haven't tried this place yet, and Isadora told me the food is really good. Plus, they've got great sangrias, I hear. I know how you like them."

When I looked over at the red light, his blue eyes glittered in the streetlights. A pink flush streaked his high cheekbones.

"Is that okay with you?"

He stared at me as if he didn't know me. Perhaps in this minute he didn't. He was accustomed to me being the assertive and gruff friend who told him what to do. Not the polite and inquisitive date who asked gentle questions.

"Yeah, JJ," he finally said softly, "that's fine with me."

Gulping down a myriad of emotions that swung from stark hunger to sheer terror in milliseconds, I drove the rest of the way without saying a word.

That in itself was unlike me. Unlike us. He sensed something different, and I was perfectly okay with that. Again, I wanted to ease into this though. I didn't want to just smash him with my feelings like a sledgehammer.

I did open the door of Gris Gris for him and told the hostess, "Reservations under Jeremy Breaux."

I ignored Charlie's stare then. When had I ever made reservations for dinner for us? Oh, right; that would be never. The hostess guided us upstairs and seated us at a nice table near the glass wall that overlooked the balcony and Magazine.

"Here you are. Your server Beth will be right with you."

Once seated, Charlie clasped his hands on the table and leaned forward and said, "Okay. What the hell is going on, JJ? Is this to make up for the way you've been treating me the past few weeks."

"How have I been treating you?" I asked, suddenly panicking. Had he noticed my change in behavior without me knowing it?

He looked down at the menu. "You know. Ignoring me and putting me off."

"I haven't been doing that."

He arched an eyebrow at me with that snarky look, and goddamn, I wanted to reach across the table and bite that sassy mouth.

Shit.

Scowling down at the menu, I replied, "Maybe I have. But I'm sorry. I didn't mean to do that."

Not really. I just couldn't stand the thought of hearing him talk about how amazing his new boyfriend Thomas was. The funny thing was that he never mentioned Thomas at all. Unless I brought him up.

Well, tonight I wanted to talk about him. But not yet. I needed to do something else first. I reached into my pocket and pulled out the long envelope right as the server popped up. I jumped and kept the envelope under the table. Charlie frowned, which I ignored.

"Hi, can I—"

"Yeah, two sangrias while we look over the menu. Thank you," I spat out, heart pumping at an erratic speed.

She paused before saying, "I'll get that right away." Then she disappeared like I'd hoped.

"What if I wanted wine tonight?" Charlie smirked.

"You never want wine unless you're eating steak. They do have a nice filet mignon here though. I'll order a glass of Cabernet if that's what you choose."

He stared and blinked at me like he didn't know me. I didn't give him long to process that all of my behavior was firmly out of the friendzone. I set the envelope on the table in front of him.

"I got you something."

He glanced from the envelope to me then back to the envelope like it was a rattlesnake about to jump up and bite him.

"Why?"

Licking my extraordinarily dry lips—where was that drink—I said, "Because I wanted to get you something."

Charlie's expression of confusion—the one he'd worn from the second I'd shown up at his apartment door—vanished and was replaced by something close to shock. Or maybe fear. My knee started bouncing under the table.

"It's not my birthday, JJ," he said in that soft voice that lacked the aggressive confidence he typically wore so well.

"I wanted to give it to you early."

Because I needed to give him time to process everything and so he could request time off from work in May around his birthday and to plan. He liked to plan. I knew that about him. I knew everything about him.

He stared at it with hesitation, his fingers a little shaky as he picked it up.

I didn't necessarily want his self-assurance to wane, but the fact that the reality of what was going on seemed to be dawning on him boosted my courage. I sat up straighter and leaned with my forearms on the table.

"Go on...open it."

Tentatively, he broke the seal and pulled out the folded piece of paper—a screenshot of my confirmation of our plane tickets for this summer. His jaw slackened as he stared at the paper.

"JJ." Then those wide blue eyes left the paper to stare at me.

"We've talked about going for years. But there never was a good time." I swallowed the lump of trepidation that he would refuse the gift. "Life slips by fast, Charlie. I think it's time."

I was talking about more than our dream trip to England and Scotland. I saw the spark of recognition in those ocean blue eyes I knew so well.

His throat worked as he swallowed. "But this is so expensive." He let out a surprised laugh. One of disbelief.

"I have a good amount in savings. Hell, I never take off work. And you know I get good tips." I gave him a sexy smile. "I want to take you. I want to do this with you. Finally." I halted my instinct to reach across the table and hold his hand. Too soon.

"I don't know what to say."

"Well, that's a first."

He laughed. "You ass." He rubbed the corner of the paper with his thumb and middle finger. A nervous tic.

"What?" I asked. "Is it Thomas?"

I couldn't even think about him still being with Thomas by the time we took this vacation we'd dreamed about taking for years. Still, I couldn't rule out the fact that he might have feelings for him and wouldn't want to go without his new boyfriend.

That queasy sensation I got every time I thought about him with Thomas returned ten-fold, lacerating my hope, sliver by sliver.

His brow pursed into a frown. "No." But then he

didn't explain further. He simply stared across the table in a state of disbelief.

"Here you are," said our server, setting down our drinks. "Can I start you off with an appetizer?"

"Sorry," I apologized. "Not just yet. Still looking."

Neither of us had spared more than a cursory glanced at the menu. Charlie reached for his drink and took a long drag with his straw. My gaze snagged on his mouth and my thoughts headed south, like all the blood in my body.

I turned my gaze to the menu but not my attention. Charlie had it all. Every single trembling ounce of my focus homed in on him. His smallest reaction—shift in expression or posture or breathing—was a signal I had to read accurately. I had to know if my Charlie was finally getting the message and whether he wanted to take this chance with me or not.

CHAPTER 6

~CHARLIE~

WHAT WAS *HAPPENING* RIGHT NOW? This felt like a date. *Was this a date?*

I stared blindly down at the menu, checking out the entrees. He'd suggested I try the chargrilled filet mignon. It was served in an oyster dressing with roasted onions and a red wine demi-glace. He was right. This was definitely something I'd choose on a menu. It also happened to be the most expensive choice.

He'd picked me up at my door, ordered my drink, bought me a gift. My head was spinning, because this certainly felt like a fucking date.

"So tell me about you and Thomas."

Maybe not a date.

Clearing my throat, I took a sip of the sangria. He was right about the drink too. It was a good one. "We're fine, I guess."

"What does that mean?" he asked with razor-sharp focus. JJ observed everything with keen awareness but usually in a subtle way that put people at ease. He wasn't being subtle right now. And I was *not* at ease. "You guess. What's the problem?"

I didn't say there was a problem, but there was. There so was.

Fine.

"We get along well. We have mutual interests. We're compatible."

JJ watched me. "But?"

"But there's just something missing."

"What's missing?" he asked, serious and grave.

"I think it's a certain chemistry actually. On my part, at least."

His hazel eyes darkened. "Chemistry is important." His voice was a raspy roll.

"It is."

That observant gaze trailed over my face with such slow progress that I felt like I was melting under the fiery sweep from my eyes to my cheeks to my mouth. A *long* time on my mouth. By the time he met my gaze again, the hazel was eaten by the black of his dilated pupils.

Never in my life had JJ looked at me like that. I felt like I was under one of the Savoie's spells, entranced and unable to move until he released me. It didn't seem as if he planned on releasing me. I'm fairly sure he wouldn't have if Beth hadn't popped up to take our order.

JJ clenched his jaw before glancing down at the menu for about three seconds before he asked me, "The filet?"

I nodded. He ordered my dinner along with a glass of Cabernet Sauvignon then the sugarcane seared duck for himself. By the time Beth swept away with our menus, JJ had seemed to return to something of his normal self.

In other words, he'd stopped looking at me like he'd rather devour me than anything on the menu. Then he took out his phone and opened some pics to show me some places to stay in the countryside of England and Scotland. He'd contacted a travel agent and had her working on our trip.

We settled into a more comfortable conversation, both of us excited about seeing so many places we'd dreamed about going to together. I couldn't believe he'd bought us tickets. He'd given me the tickets as a—what—an early birthday gift?

After a fabulous dinner, which JJ insisted on paying for, my mind strayed again to the fact that this felt different. JJ wasn't treating me like his friend. Far from it. And when he opened the door to Isaac's gallery and placed a firm hand at my nape to usher me in gently, my whole body broke out into a sweat.

But that wasn't the worst. He tortured me the entire night. When I stood in front of a piece to soak in the painting, he'd stand right behind me. Never quite touching, but the heat of his big body radiated to mine, making me want to lean back into his arms. Unless someone passed too closely, then he'd wrap a hand on my hip and move me gently to one side. It was maddening bliss. An explosion of desire held me captive and orbited around the two of us. I had no idea what to do.

So I did nothing. Just observed the exhibit quietly and refused to chat with Isaac too long, especially when he asked if I was feeling ill.

"Just hot," I'd said, which had Isaac sending his assistant to check the thermostat. It wasn't the temperature in the room, of course. But the internal temperature of my body with JJ's unwavering attentiveness at my side.

JJ fetched me a glass of water when I said I was thirsty. Because I was sweating like mad at JJ's close proximity and heated attention and subtle touches. All night long.

"Ready to go?" he asked softly from behind me, his mouth brushing my ear.

Fuck!

I shivered. "Yeah."

This was all so bizarre. I wasn't the quiet one. I typically had a million things to say at these exhibits, detailing my love of shape in one painting or my distaste of drab colors in another. And the strangest part of all is that JJ didn't comment a word about my unusual behavior. That's because he was too busy revving my libido up to scorching levels and pretending this was the most common thing in the world.

"You don't have to come up," I told him when he parked along St. Charles and got out of the Jeep with me.

"You don't want me to?" he asked as he came around to my side.

"It's not that."

He was now standing in front of me, clenching his jaw, my back to the passenger side door of his Jeep.

"What is it?" His voice was hard, rough, edged with agitation.

I scoffed, staring up at him, trying to figure out what the fuck was going on. "JJ, I'm not sure what—"

His mouth was on mine, his body crushing me

against the car. I whimpered at the onslaught of sensation of JJ's firm but soft mouth devouring mine. The brush of his beard made me rock hard. He groaned and bit my bottom lip, sucked it into his mouth then gripped my nape and angled me so he could go deeper.

I curled my hands into his shirt at his back, trying to hold on as he devoured me with ravenous need. When he stroked his tongue against mine, I jerked in his arms. His hand at my hip scooped to my ass where he squeezed while fucking my mouth with his tongue.

It was the most erotic moment of my life, and I still had all my clothes on. He pressed his pelvis against me, his hard dick crushed against my stomach. I never thought in all my life I'd feel the heady sensation of the hard steel pipe JJ carried around in his pants. I'd had many a moment to observe him in near nakedness to know that he was well-endowed. But I hadn't believed I'd ever feel him against me, pressed hard with a desperate grind.

I whimpered again, then nipped at his lips with my teeth before licking back inside.

"Fuck, Charlie," he groaned and thrust his hips against me, the rubbing friction against my hard dick not enough.

"What's happening?" I murmured, lost in the oblivion of his hot mouth and hard body.

His hand on my ass trailed to the front as he coasted

his mouth down my throat, biting me along the way. Not licking or kissing but *biting* me. I thought I might come right then and there, then he wrapped his hand around my dick through my pants and squeezed.

Through the fog of burning lust, a flicker of sanity and reality pierced through the haze.

"Thomas," I said.

He stopped abruptly, heaving breaths, and then pressed his forehead to my shoulder, removing his hand from my dick. He knew I wasn't calling him Thomas. There was no way I'd accidently mistake him for Thomas.

"I'm still with him," I whispered, panting, hardly able to catch my breath.

I wanted to run upstairs, grab my butcher knife and stab myself. Everything I'd ever wanted was happening right here, right now, but I wasn't sure exactly what brought on this change. And I couldn't let it go further while I was still with another guy. My heart may not be committed to Thomas, but I wouldn't betray him either. Not like this.

I wanted to talk with JJ about what had just happened and figure it all out, but he pulled his body away from mine. I felt the loss keenly. He cupped my face and eased in, eyes burning like stars gone supernova. He pressed a gentle kiss to my lips, breaking my heart with the tender touch.

"Sorry," he murmured, his voice all rust and gravel.

I closed my eyes, heart breaking that he seemed to be regretting what had just happened.

"Look at me." His dominant command had my eyes snapping open and body hardening even more. "I'm not sorry for doing this. But my timing is bad. That's not what I intended." His dark gaze dropped to my mouth and he swept his thumb across my bottom lip before clenching his jaw. "We'll talk when you're ready."

Then he marched around the car, got in his Jeep, and drove away, leaving me standing there like a lovestruck fool.

"What in the *hell* just happened?"

CHAPTER 7

~JJ~

SLAMMING THE DOOR, I stormed into my kitchen, whipped open the refrigerator door, pulled out a beer, twisted off the cap, and guzzled the entire bottle without stopping. I tossed the empty bottle in the trash and grabbed another, drinking this one a little slower as I made my way into the living room and sank onto the couch.

Miko walked into the room, tail swaying high, then jumped onto the back of the sofa and sniffed at my hand since my arm was braced along the sofa back.

"I shouldn't have done that, Miko." I scratched her head. She let me for a minute then curled up out of reach and watched me with that superior air of hers. "It was perfect. Fucking perfect. Then I looked at his mouth and I lost my goddamn mind."

Meow.

"I know, I know. I tried! But, my God! He's so beautiful. And smart. And sexy and when I look at him now, my heart just slips away from me. And apparently so does my brain."

I took another gulp of beer, sitting in the dim light from the kitchen.

Meow.

"It's not stupid. I just have to try again. Go about this differently."

I stared at the wall, drank my beer, and beat myself up for losing complete and total control.

But it felt—*fuck!*—so goddamn good. To hold him. Touch him. Kiss him.

I let my head drop to the sofa and shifted my hard dick in my pants. Sighing at my failure at date night, I relished the thought that Charlie had responded to me. He felt everything I had. He was as undone as me.

Knock, knock, knock.

Frowning, I set my beer on the coffee table and crossed to the back door, noticing Charlie's car in the driveway.

My stomach flipped as I jerked the door open.

He'd changed into jeans and a cotton V-neck and

put on his gray peacoat. His hair was mussed, and he looked amazing. My heart lurched, trying to leap right out of my chest, like I hadn't just seen him thirty minutes ago.

"May I come in?" he asked softly, eyes wide and imploring.

"Of course." I moved out of the way since I was blocking his entrance like an idiot. I was still dumbfounded why he'd come over so soon after...well, after I'd mauled him on the street.

He walked in and sat on the sofa, giving Miko a stroke before turning back to me. I remained standing, hands in my pants pockets.

He noted the beer on the table before asking, "Why did you kiss me?"

Unable to respond because I thought it was pretty damn obvious, I moved closer and sat on the coffee table facing him. But before I could find the right words, he went on, nervous tension in his voice.

"Was it because you don't like Thomas? Or...what exactly were you thinking?"

Propping my elbows on my thighs, I leaned forward, staring at him while he kept his back straight, his gaze steady on me.

"No," I stated definitively. "I don't like Thomas. I fucking *hate* Thomas."

"Why?"

"Because he gets to be with you."

He started breathing faster. I wanted to reach out and touch him, assure him that what I felt was real. That I wasn't just being an overbearing best friend having a lapse in sanity or that all of this was simply because I was jealous. Though admittedly, I was seething with envy.

But if I touched him right now, I knew it would be all over. I'd be on him in a heartbeat. I couldn't trust myself. I needed to get the words out, make him understand. And hope to all things holy that he felt the same way. That I wasn't alone in this.

"The reason I kissed you is because you're my whole world, Charlie. You're my best friend. But I realized something recently. I want more." My voice dropped into a deeper register. "I want you to be my lover. I want everything. I want all of you."

Silence except for his quick breathing, his blue eyes broadcasting exactly what I was hoping for. Acceptance. Longing. Deep, deep want.

"Okay."

Raising my brow, I asked, "Okay?"

"I called Thomas after you left." He licked his lips, stirring my desire to full attention. "I broke up with him."

I gripped the backs of his knees and tugged him forward, so I could cup his beautiful face and bring his mouth to mine. "That's the best fucking news I've heard in ages," I ground out against his lips.

He wrapped his hands around my wrists, voice trembling when he said, "I've wanted this for a long time, JJ." He squeezed my wrists. "This. Us."

I pressed a soft kiss to that beautiful mouth, coaxing his lips apart. He moaned when I swept my tongue inside. Softly, gently. All the while my blood was burning. I pulled us apart and waited till he opened his eyes, till I had his full attention.

"Now you're mine." The timbre of my voice was grating and rough. Dominant.

"Not yet," he said in that snarky voice that made a beeline straight to my dick. A challenge flickered in his eyes.

I bit his bottom lip between my teeth then trailed my tongue to soothe it. "Well, let's do something about that."

Miko twitched her tail and caught my attention, watching us like a fucking pervert. I didn't want an audience for this.

I stood, taking Charlie's hand, and led him to my bedroom. Something I thought I'd never do. I could feel him trembling when I turned and removed his coat then tossed it to the side.

He closed his eyes and blew out a shaky breath. I pushed him down to sit on the edge of the bed then I knelt in front of him. I was bigger and taller than Charlie and my bed sat low to the ground, so we were eye-to-eye in this position.

"Easy," I murmured soothingly, leaning forward and grazing my mouth up his neck, which had the opposite effect of calming him. I wrapped a hand along the other side, stroking the front of his throat with my thumb. "I'm going to take care of you, baby."

He made a whimpering sound in his throat but said nothing. His hands found my shoulders, holding tight as I licked a path back to his mouth. I couldn't help the groan rumbling in my chest when he teased his tongue inside my mouth. The fact that this was Charlie—*my* Charlie—making my cock rock-hard with a tentative swipe of his tongue had my hands moving faster.

I stripped off his shirt, roving a palm down the lean muscle of his chest and torso till I was unsnapping and unzipping his jeans with remarkable speed, still kissing his sweet mouth.

"I need to taste you, baby," I murmured.

He made that needy sound in the back of his throat again, making my cock twitch. While I worked on getting his jeans and boxer briefs off, he pulled at the hem of my shirt. I sat back for a split second, unbuttoned it the rest of the way and tossed it aside. He froze, chest heaving, staring at my torso while I eased his boxers down his legs.

I couldn't help but smile at the lust blazing in those pretty blue eyes. But my attention refocused fast on his hard dick flush against his stomach. My mouth watered. He was so beautiful. So perfectly proportioned. All lean and hard and pleasing to my lusty gaze.

Without hesitation, I wrapped my hand around him and gave it a smooth stroke.

"Oh, God," he groaned, his head falling back.

"Lay all the way back," I planted a hand to his chest and urged him backward on the bed. "Spread wider for me."

Gripping a thigh with my free hand, I pushed it wide. He let his other fall open till his knees hit the edge of the mattress.

"Just like that," I murmured soothingly, watching my hand stroke him slowly while I reached over to the nightstand.

He didn't even open his eyes, panting faster. I swear, I'd never seen Charlie this silent his entire life. I grinned at how overwhelmed he was, understanding that feeling completely. After I opened the drawer and pulled out the oil Devraj had given me, I let go of his dick long enough to pour some oil on my palm and rub it evenly on both palms and fingers. I instantly felt the heat blooming in my hands.

Settling further between Charlie's open thighs, I

gripped him at the base and swallowed him till he hit the back of my throat.

The sound Charlie made was borderline feral and frightening, like an animal caught in a desperate, dangerous situation. I moaned at the salty taste of him, my cock a painful throb in my pants.

His hips canted up and his hands fisted in my hair. I growled, taking him deeper, sucking hard at the crown and stroking the base.

"Jeremy," he hissed, rocking his hips and squirming.

I cupped his sac and massaged the oil in good while I deep-throated his cock.

"What in the—fuck—JJ—holy *fuck*!"

I moaned as his arousal reached a fever pitch, then I slid my middle finger down to his ass and circled the tight hole, oiling him good before I pushed it inside him.

"JJ!" He fisted my hair so hard, my scalp burned, which only turned me on more.

I had no idea it would feel this fucking good. And I hadn't even gotten my cock inside him yet. I dragged my tongue along the underside of his thick dick and stroked him hard from base to tip.

"I want you to come in my mouth, Charlie. Give me what I want."

Then I thrust two fingers into his ass right as I sucked him down again. He bucked his hips and hot come spurted into my mouth. I fisted him hard and sucked the crown of his dick as he came hard and fast, his thighs trembling. When his tight hold in my hair loosened and he relaxed into the bed, I stood up and unfastened my pants.

His eyes were mere slits, his expression blissed out from the orgasm as he watched me strip for him. Once naked, I gripped my thick cock and gave it a heavy stroke. His eyes widened then. I didn't want him to suck me off. I needed to be inside him. His gaze remained on my thickening dick.

"I want to be inside you, Charlie," I murmured low, still stroking myself, sweeping my thumb across the crown.

He scooted further up to the headboard and lay down then spread his legs wide, knees up. I didn't think I could get any harder, but this was fucking ridiculous. His easy submission had my balls tightening with need.

"Don't worry," I rumbled, reaching for the oil. "I'll be gentle."

"I'm not worried," he murmured, voice so raspy and sexy I felt it stroke along my skin like a physical caress. "I've imagined this for a long time. I've wanted it for longer."

I gulped hard at the vulnerable expression on his face, which tapped hard on my heart. Before I got so worked up that I came in my hand, I pulled a condom from the drawer and rolled it on quickly then oiled myself up. Crawling up the bed between his open legs, I pressed my body down to his, chest to chest, and looked into the clear eyes of the person I knew better than anyone on this earth. The one I loved more than anyone as well.

I tried to bat back the jealousy of earlier, but I needed to know one thing. It wouldn't change anything, but I still needed to know.

I brushed my lips against his, swiping my tongue along his lower lip. "Did you let Thomas fuck you?"

"No."

"Did you fuck him?"

The devil smiled at me. "No."

When I frowned, he added, "All I could ever think about was you."

I pressed my forehead to his and reached between us to line up my dick to his entrance. He jumped.

"It's okay," I whispered against his mouth, gripping his thigh, gently bending his leg higher. "I promise to go slow."

"It's not that." He chuckled. "It just already feels so good." He dragged his blunt nails across my upper back, the other hand slid into my hair. "All of you just feels so good."

I sank into his kiss then I sank into his body. Nice and slow, because I was aware of my size. I didn't want to hurt him. He groaned into my mouth when my hips met the flesh of his ass. He clenched and cursed as I pulled out to the tip and stroked back in.

"Good?" I asked, holding his gaze, making sure no pain was etched there.

"Amazing," he breathed, then his eyes rolled closed and I started fucking him with nice, deep strokes.

His own dick was rousing again. I pressed down harder, wanting to feel the slide of his skin against mine as I pumped inside him. I buried my mouth against his neck and sucked and licked and bit. He arched his neck for me, giving me better access to his throat.

"Harder, JJ," he moaned.

I latched my mouth onto the curve of his shoulder and neck and pounded his ass, my balls slapping with every thrust.

"So good, so good," he whispered, digging his fingers into my back.

He clenched his ass and that did me in. I drove deep and roared into his neck as I came so fucking hard I saw spots at the edge of my vision.

Charlie held me hard then caressed my hair when I remained tense and immobile on top of him. My body slowly loosed its rigid hold, my dick softening inside him when I shifted up onto my forearms.

He was grinning with that mischievous look he so often wore in life.

"What?" I asked.

"It was better than I ever thought it would be."

"How long have you been thinking about this?"

He shrugged a shoulder. "Years."

"*Years*?" I bellowed.

"You're kind of oblivious, JJ."

"Why didn't you ever tell me?"

He got shy again, averting his gaze. I lifted a finger under his chin and forced him to look at me. "Why?" I demanded.

He narrowed his eyes then finally said, "Because I couldn't lose you as a friend. If you didn't feel the same way about me."

I understood that feeling, but I wondered if he'd said something if we might've given this a go a lot sooner.

"I could've been fucking this sweet ass for years, but you were too afraid to tell me?" A flush of pink crested his cheeks. I grinned and lowered my mouth to kiss him softly. "That's okay. I forgive you. But I have a lot of lost time to make up for."

He laughed, tightening his hold on me. We kissed for a while longer, his dick growing harder against my stomach.

I lifted up and went to the bathroom to take care of the condom and wash up. When I came back and climbed under the covers where he was now, I pulled him onto my chest and stroked a palm over his hip.

"Let's rest a minute then I'll take care of you."

"What do you mean?" he snuggled closer, throwing a leg over mine. "You already did."

I grunted agreement. "I want to feel you inside me, Charlie."

He blew out a heavy sigh.

"What?" I asked.

He tightened his arm around my waist. "I just never thought I'd ever hear you say something like that to me."

I squeezed his hip. "Well, get used to it. I'm going to be demanding."

"Yes, sir," he sassed.

"Fuck, Charlie. You're going to get me hard again, talking like that."

He laughed then I closed my eyes to rest them for just a minute.

CHAPTER 8

~CHARLIE~

I WOKE up to being practically smothered under JJ's weight. We'd both fallen asleep before we could go for round two last night. I think we were both emotionally and physically exhausted.

Currently, he was spooning me from behind with a heavy leg and arm over me. And while it was probably one of the best ways that I'd ever woken up, I needed the bathroom and a shower.

Sliding out from underneath him, I walked softly into his bathroom and shut the door. I pulled out my toothbrush from the second drawer where I kept it for the times I crashed on his sofa. That hadn't been in a while, but my toothbrush was still right where I left it, which made me smile. JJ had never let another man put his things in his house. He'd never had long relationships at all, frankly.

That had me wondering if maybe his subconscious was waiting for me all along and he never realized it. I turned on the shower and stepped inside, loving that he'd remodeled this older home with modern fixtures. For example, this shower was nice and big, with a giant showerhead and floor-to-ceiling tiles, and a wide indention for shampoos and soap products.

While I relished the hot water pouring over me, I felt a shift in the air. JJ had come in and was brushing his teeth. I wanted to laugh at how he acted like it was the most normal thing in the world to walk into his bathroom and find me naked in his shower. Before I could think much past that, he slid the glass door open and walked in behind me.

Turning so that the shower was hitting my back, I smiled up at him, "Good morning."

JJ usually wore his stoic and grave face, but today there was a definite tilt of naughty to his mouth. It paired well with the wicked gleam in his eyes.

"Oh, it's about to be."

That's when I noticed that he'd brought in that oil from last night and set it on the shelf. Before I could ask him about it, he cradled my head and kissed the hell out of me, delving deep with his tongue. I gripped his shoulders to hang on while he devoured me on a groan.

Damn, I'd never known how sexy JJ truly was. I'd spent an infinite number of hours watching him move behind the bar at The Cauldron, his sexy, gruff expression fixed in place as he handled customers efficiently, looking devastatingly handsome in his own grumpy way. But JJ in action? With a mission toward orgasms? That was on another level entirely.

His big hands coasted down my body; stroking and squeezing until he wrapped his palm around my cock.

I gasped at the incredible sensation of his rough hand taking control of me. It was more divine than I ever could've imagined. His other hand coasted back up till he gripped my nape. He broke the kiss, his eyes dark and fierce.

"I want you inside me, Charlie."

I reached down and gripped his hard cock, already long and thick and ready to go. I loved having him inside me last night. I wouldn't have minded having him fuck me again first, because for heaven's sake the man knew how to fuck.

"JJ, I can—"

He let go of me, picked up the bottle of oil, and swept every other soap and shampoo bottle to the floor. Damn, he was aggressive. My cock got harder at his intensity. He poured some oil into his palm and stroked my cock.

I flinched and closed my eyes at the sensation of the oil heating and penetrating my skin, tantalizing my arousal to new heights.

He dipped his head lower, pressing his lips to mine. "Come fuck me, Charlie," he whispered.

Opening my eyes, I asked. "Did you bring a condom?"

He shook his head, eyes never leaving mine. "You're clean. I'm clean. I was too much in a hurry to stop for a conversation last night, but I don't want to use one. If you're okay with it."

It's true that we got tested frequently. And I knew he hadn't been with anyone since our last check-up. Neither had I.

I simply nodded.

That sexy smile tilted higher, then he leaned one forearm on the tiled shelf and stroked his dick with the other.

"No foreplay, huh?" I teased, gliding my hands down his muscular back, my eyes on that tight curvy prize.

"Need you now, baby," he said gruffly, hardening my dick more with that endearment.

I took the oil and lubed my fingers then circled his tight hole before stroking inside.

"Holy fuuuuuck," growled JJ, dropping his forehead to his forearm while pumping his hand on his dick.

I remembered that sensation last night when he lubed me with this oil. It must be some magical concoction or something. I'd find out later, because we needed shelves of this shit.

Once he was loosened up and moaning in pleasure, I squeezed his shoulder where I had a good grip on him then drove my cock inside him.

"Oh, hell," I muttered, gripping his other shoulder so I wouldn't fall down as my knees buckled.

I froze, basking in the heady sensation of being buried balls deep inside the man I loved.

"Charlie," he ground out roughly, "if you don't start moving, I'm going to turn around and fuck you against the wall."

That wasn't much of a threat, but it did wake me up. So I did as I was told and fucked him. I'd say I was embarrassed at how aroused I was and how quickly I felt my orgasm building, but the fact was that it was a damn miracle I could hold out at all.

JJ was the sexiest man I'd ever known. But he was also the most intense, the most caring, the most compassionate. And all of my feelings about him and the fact that I was inside of him raced me toward a climax I couldn't prevent even if I tried.

I reached around and gripped my hand above his,

both of us stroking his dick while I pounded him harder. His cock was hot and throbbing, pulling a feral groan from my throat.

"So perfect," I mumbled right before I came with a rough shout.

"Yes," hissed JJ, still stroking himself.

My hand had fallen lax at my side. I pulled out of him and fell to my knees, grabbing hold of his hips and shoving at him to turn around.

He did, his hot gaze on my mouth as he stepped forward and fed his dick between my lips.

"Fuck, yes, baby."

I took as much of him as I could, looking up at his fierce scowl as he pumped his hips. He cradled my face but gave me shallow thrusts as he slid his thumb to the underside of his cock, caressing along my mouth, feeling himself slide inside of me.

"Just like that," he murmured.

I put both hands on his thick thighs and dug my fingers into his flesh then I sucked hard.

"You want it?" he growled.

I gave a quick nod still sucking him hard.

Then he was coming down my throat. He dropped his head back, his Adam's apple bobbing on a deep groan before he whispered, "Fuck, I love you."

I kept sucking him all down through the orgasm, tears welling in my eyes. Not from him thrusting too deep but from the insane emotions exploding in my chest. Did he just mean that?

He pulled out of my mouth and scooped me off my feet under my arms. I kept forgetting how strong he was. It wasn't like I was a waif of a man, but JJ was so much bigger.

Pulling me into his arms, he brushed his mouth across my cheek, breathing hard, holding me harder. Buoying up my courage, I asked, "Was that just orgasmic bliss? What you said?"

He pulled back, cupping my head. "No." Then he pressed his lips to mine with the softest, gentlest kiss I'd ever felt in my life. Holding my gaze, he said clearly in that low, rumbly timbre, "I love you."

Heart frantically trying to beat out of my ribcage, voice cracking a little, I told him, "I love you, too."

Then he smiled tenderly, turned me around and proceeded to wash my hair and body, melting me into a ball of mush. I tried not to fixate too much on how insanely good this felt, too afraid I'd blink and it would all disappear. But one thing I knew about JJ, he didn't do things in half-measures. And he didn't do anything until he'd made a good, sound decision. So the fact that he'd fucked me good and was now petting and caring for me like I was his lover told me that he was all in.

Then he spanked me on the ass and said, "All done. Go get dressed."

Laughing, I climbed out, catching sight of that oil. "Where the hell did you get that sex oil?"

"Devraj gave it to me."

"When?" I grabbed a towel. "And why?"

"When I went over to their house and told Isadora that I wanted you. That I loved you."

He said it so matter of fact. Meanwhile, my heart was doing cartwheels inside my chest.

"You told her?"

He slid the glass door open, shampoo suds in his hair and beard. I swear, he was so adorable. "I want everyone to know you're mine."

That fierce glint was back. His possessive streak was doing all kinds of insane things to my libido. I wrapped the towel around my waste and used his brush for my hair.

"Don't take too long, beautiful," he said. "I want to go to Sunday dinner with the Savoies."

"But they'll know if they see us together today."

There was no way in hell I was going to be able to hide my feelings now.

"I told you already. I want everyone to know we're together." He turned off the faucet and prowled out, grabbing a towel and drying his hair first.

I couldn't help my wandering gaze down his unbelievable body, all beaded with water.

"You have a problem with people knowing?" He toweled off his chest.

"Not at all."

Then he caught me staring.

"Charlie."

"What?"

"Go get dressed unless you want me to bend you over that sink right now."

"You say these things like they're actual threats."

Laughing, he walked over to me and gave me a quick, hard kiss. "We have the rest of our lives now. Let's go eat dinner with the family." Then he walked into the bedroom.

The Savoies were our family, and I couldn't wait to tell Violet and Evie. Even if it was so new and made me strangely shy. I mean, I wasn't shy about anything, but JJ threw me completely off balance. I wondered how long it would take me to get used to our new relationship. JJ acted like we'd always been lovers. Like none of this was a big, fucking deal. It was a very big deal to me!

He returned from the bedroom, his towel wrapped around his waist, while I stood dazed in front of the mirror. He stood behind me, easing his hands around my hips over the towel. He dropped his lips to my shoulder, watching me in the reflection.

"You okay?"

I nodded woodenly.

"You don't seem okay." He trailed his mouth up to the side of my neck, his bristles tickling my skin.

I shivered. "It's just all so..."

He grinned, his thumb brushing above the towel to caress my skin. "I know, baby. But it's for real."

"I know."

He stood to his full height, reaching his left hand up to cover my heart. "I really do love you, Charlie."

"I really do love you," I said, still breathless.

He kissed my cheek. "Go get dressed. It'll get easier."

I suppose it would. But one thing I knew for sure, my love for this man, my best friend, would only grow more.

❄

Five Months Later

"CAN you believe we're standing here?" JJ stood beside me, hands braced on the brick of the parapet of Alnwick Castle in England.

"Yes," I answered him. "I knew we'd eventually do this. What I can't believe is that I'm standing here next to my boyfriend. And that he gave me a blow job right before we left our hotel."

He wrapped a hand around my shoulder and pulled

me into his embrace, pressing a kiss to my temple. "Then you're really not going to believe what I'm going to do to you after dinner tonight."

Laughing, I threw my arm around his waist and enjoyed the sunset view of the grounds of Alnwick.

"So here we stand, where one of the scenes of Downton Abbey took place." I sighed happily, reminiscing our rewatch of the show before we took this trip.

"And where scenes from Harry Potter One and Two were filmed."

"Really? How'd you know that? You researched?"

He laughed. "Evie told me. She researched herself and was quite happy to see us visiting a place that played as the grounds of Hogwarts in a few movies."

"Not shocking."

"Mmm."

"I'm a little concerned about her."

"I would be too if her man wasn't so protective."

"She's awfully big."

"That happens when you've got three babies in your belly."

That thought had my brain straying to something I'd been thinking about lately. "JJ?"

"Hm?"

"Do you want kids someday?"

He turned his head down to me and smiled. "Yeah. Do you?"

"Not now," I rushed to say. "But one day. Yeah."

He dipped his head and kissed me softly, teasing his tongue into my mouth. "You'll be a great father," he whispered.

"So will you."

We shared a contented smile, the kind that I understood only came between two people deeply in love. Because I'd never experienced this sort of smile, this sort of feeling, before JJ.

Then we watched the sun sinking in reds and golds along the horizon of Northumberland, enjoying one of many adventures that life had in store for us.

YOU'RE A MEAN ONE, MR. GRIM

❄

Timeline: Takes place during the same time as* **Witches Get Stitches.

CHAPTER 1

~LIVVY~

I WAS PRETTY SURE the guy sitting across from me was a robot. Seriously. He hadn't blinked in the last eight minutes. Nor had he looked once at any of us in the high-rise lobby. I'd been taking inventory of my competition since my arrival twenty minutes ago, and so far I was feeling fairly confident in my chances.

My attention wandered to the mini-Christmas tree on the receptionist's desk and the lights strung up artfully around the room. It was just past New Year's, so I suppose it wasn't too late to have them still up. It did make the sterile lobby cheerier. There was even holiday music pouring out of the lobby speakers above us.

It said a lot about this company and the big boss, that he'd let holiday decorations go up and stay past the due date. Another plus for CEO Victor Garrison. My gaze wandered back to those sitting in the lobby with me.

Some might say *don't judge a book by its cover* or *things aren't always what they seem,* but that's bullshit. Grandma Maybelle taught me that you could tabulate everything you needed to know within five minutes of meeting someone. Or in this case, observing, since I hadn't yet officially met the other semi-finalists sitting around me.

Take the blonde witch in a fuchsia jumpsuit and kitten heels who'd arrived second only to me. If the jumpsuit were the professional sort, I'd say she was in the running. But it was a sexy jumpsuit revealing an abundance of cleavage and so tight you could actually call it a cat-suit.

The condescending looks she kept throwing me also revealed she was insecure and possibly intimidated. She should be because she looked like she'd shown up to the casting call for Cat Woman not the semi-finalists interview for a PR competition sponsored by the prestigious Garrison Media Corporation. With a grand prize of $100,000 to be invested in the winner's new business venture. The association with GMC and mentorship by its top minds along with the prestige and publicity of being the winner could make a world of difference.

Sorry, Kitty-cat. You're out.

Then there were the three well-dressed vampires wearing serious suits and serious faces. They'd arrived within a minute of each other and lined the wall next to me, giving polite nods, while sizing me and Kitty-cat up. One of the vamps examined Kitty-cat and me as if we'd be potential fuck-buddies, but the other two gave us brief once-overs then dismissed us to stare off into space.

I was accustomed to being underestimated by men because of my looks. I won't moan and groan and say it's a hardship being pretty, but I will definitely admit that it's sometimes an obstacle.

For some insane reason, many men—and females for that matter—liked to put women in two categories. Pretty or intelligent. Apparently, being both is considered an anomaly. And the prettier you are, the less likely it is that you also have an above average IQ. I've spent my life enjoying enlightening people how wrong they were.

After the trio of vamps, two more professionally attired women arrived one after the other, barely glancing our way, taking seats next to Kitty-cat. One of them eyed me with disdain. A vampire. I wondered what I'd done, but then she did the same to the three amigos along the wall next to me.

No telling whether she was putting on her tough face to boost her own confidence or whether she just hated all people in general.

The other woman, a witch giving me Aura vibes, was a brunette who appeared to be in her twenties, probably the youngest here. She smiled politely then kept her gaze on her clasped hands in her lap.

Then finally, Mr. Robot had arrived and plopped his ass down across from me but didn't appear to acknowledge that there were any other humans in the room. He was a warlock, but I wasn't sure what kind. Very hard to read, this one.

With one minute left to the actual arrival time, I focused on the door leading into the CEO's office, realizing there were just eight of us in the semi-final round. According to the contest rules and regulations, there should be nine semi-finalists.

CEO of GMC Victor Garrison was a highly respected businessman, but also an affluent and powerful warlock. This contest was open to supernaturals only. He'd advertised through the SuperNet for the contest, and the second I saw it, I felt a sizzle of magic buzz through my blood. I knew I was meant to be a part of this.

We'd competed in the first round, which consisted of us giving a five-minute pitch of a supernatural cause of our choice via live video feed to the CEO and his contest panel.

This wouldn't have been so nerve-wracking if we hadn't had to do the video in the same room with all of the contestants watching on. I had a feeling they added that high-pressure situation as part of the first test, which I'd passed brilliantly I might add. An audience never cowed me. Rather, the extra stress energized me to perform better.

We'd been selected based on our portfolios and business proposals plus the live video. After today's semi-finalist interviews, we'd be whittled down to three finalists.

The door leading to the corridor and bank of elevators opened and in stepped that mother fucking grim.

Hell to the no!

His obsidian gaze swept the room indifferently then he did a double-take on me and sauntered closer.

I glanced down at the empty seat next to me. "This seat's taken," I told him right as he stood before me, reeking of all that dark grimness that I recognized from last time.

His wide mouth tipped up on one side, revealing that insanely attractive dimple. He put both hands casually in the pockets of his perfectly pressed charcoal pants, which somehow made his broad chest, encased in a pristine starched shirt, look even more delicious.

Unlike the other men in the room, he wore a suit jacket but no tie, giving him both a I-don't-give-a-fuck attitude mixed with I've-got-this-in-the-bag.

He focused those enigmatic eyes on me, his black hair cut to business perfection though a little longer on top so that it fell over one brow when he looked down.

He swept his gaze over me from heel to head then licked his lips before saying, "You don't want me sitting next to you, Lavinia?"

Frowning at his familiar tone—and the fact that he had been digging to find out my real name since I introduced myself as Livvy at the live video interview—I kept my hand on the empty seat.

"Been doing a little light stalking, have you? How do you know my name?"

"I make a habit of knowing my competition." He glanced at the others, giving the vampires and Kitty-cat a decidedly arrogant look. "So I know four names in this room."

"Dick," muttered the vampire closest to us.

Gareth Blackwater didn't even flinch, his focus solely on me.

Yes, I knew his name too. But he did his live video right before I did at the last interview, so it was hard not to hear his name. It might've also been the fact that his grim aura affected me with unnerving intensity.

All grims radiated a dark aura, tapping into people's baser instincts and wicked urges. As a powerful Influencer, I typically could shield myself from most of their aura. But this guy's signature carried a punch of enormous magical power. There was also the fact that I did not care for the one emotion he evoked anytime he was near me.

Burning, brain-scattering lust.

He grinned at me now as if he knew it. It was almost as if he reeked of one of Clara's love potions (that were really just all about desire, not love). But no one else seemed to be affected by him the way I was. Well, except now Kitty-cat was eye-fucking him like he was a bowl of sweet cream she wanted to lick up. And that irked the hell out of me for some reason.

"You know," I informed him haughtily, "my dad always said that if you're late, you're telling the other party that they're not worth your time."

He pulled one hand from his pocket and glanced at his expensive looking watch then back at me. "Good thing I'm right on time."

He pointed a finger at the door leading into the CEO's office right as a smart-dressed woman stepped from inside.

She scanned the room. "Okay, contestants. It's time to get started."

Gareth slid into the seat right next to me. The one I'd tried to block him from. He barely missed sitting on my hand as I snatched it off the seat.

Then he leaned closer and whispered, "See? Perfect timing."

I ground my teeth together, willing this incessant allure he wore like a cloak of sex pheromones to go away. But it wouldn't!

The businesswoman in a navy-blue pencil skirt and cream silk blouse looked down at her tablet and tapped the screen with a stylus.

"Alright. First up, we need Michael Tudor, Davian Russell, and Bitsy Lumberton." Two of the vampires—the one who was checking us out and the Shemar Moore lookalike—stood and stepped through the door, followed by Kitty-cat.

I huffed a laugh to myself, mumbling, "Of course."

"Of course they'd save the best for last?" came the conceited question from the grim sitting next to me.

"No, you arrogant ass."

"What then?"

He was completely unperturbed by my antagonistic tone. As a matter of fact, I'd think he was enjoying himself if the merry glint in his soulless eyes was a clue.

"Her name. Just seemed to match her personality."

I could feel him staring at me. "Interesting how people's names often match their appearance and personality, isn't it?"

Unable to ignore the rumbling timbre of his unnaturally deep voice, I turned to look at him. His body was angled slightly toward me, but his long-fingered hands were clasped casually in his lap. There was a tattoo on the back of one hand that I couldn't quite decipher at this angle.

I tried to find a smartass come-back or anything to say at all, but for the moment I couldn't help admiring the symmetry of his contrasting features. This close, I could see that his eyes weren't actually black, but near enough. And definitely not soulless. Deep, ebony pools a woman could drown in.

His pale skin was framed by his black hair. His features were entirely too sharp and hard to be considered beautiful, but he'd look like a fucking wet dream behind my camera lens. He had the kind of face that photographers fantasized about.

"For example," he continued in a soft purr, "Lavinia Lenore Savoie."

Those dark eyes swept over my face, caressing every curve and crevice.

"This name reminds me of endless stars in a midnight sky. Too far away to reach. Their light nothing more than an nth of the power they truly hold, casting the watcher into an abyss of wonder and maddening desire. Making him imagine what bliss he'd experience if he could only touch the untouchable."

He paused, and I couldn't breathe as his gaze dropped to my mouth.

"But the watcher knows that if he ever made his fantasy a reality, if he touched those stars, he'd be scorched to nothing but ash."

I fucking shivered.

He didn't smile at my lack of a quippy response. He simply sat back in his seat and watched the door, clenching his jaw and awaiting our turn to go inside.

What the hell was that?

Completely flustered—a state of being I had zero experience with—I stared straight ahead, trying to figure out why and how he both complimented and insulted me in the same breath. I wasn't some femme fatale if that's what he was insinuating. Asshat.

But behind all that, he'd admitted something I don't think he'd meant to. That he looked on me with *maddening desire*.

This was so not good.

CHAPTER 2

~GARETH~

I JUST COULDN'T KEEP *my fucking mouth shut, could I?*

It was her magic. The beguiling witch. She was a beacon of beauty and allure, her magic as a Warper amplifying every attractive asset she had.

And fucking hell, did she have assets. I'd never seen a woman more beautiful in all my life.

She was my rival. *Get that into your goddamn head.*

Hell, I'd be lucky to make it through this semi-final interview without a raging hard-on while sitting next to her. Somehow, I knew we'd be in the same group. Fate enjoyed torturing me that way. Dangling intense temptation in front of my face, and daring me to take the bait.

But I wouldn't. Giving into my temptation of her would be like consigning myself to some level of hell that involved torture, self-flagellation, and a lake of fire. Mind you, I enjoyed a bit of spanking and whipping now and then, but only by my own hand. I did *not* enjoy being on the other end of the lash.

But Lavinia...

An image of her blindfolded, bound, naked, and bent over my bed flashed to mind.

Stop!

I expelled the image before it could take full effect, having to shift in my seat anyway and subtly move my half-hard dick.

The assistant came out again and called three more contestants as the first group exited the waiting room. The witch in the tight outfit gave me a not-so-subtle fuck-me look as she passed. I ignored her invitation. Not interested.

Overeager and drooling wasn't my type. Defiant and brilliant was. Like the bombshell sitting next to me.

Why did Lavinia have to be blindingly gorgeous on top of being highly intelligent and charming? Her spark of bold rebellion was the icing on the cake. This woman was my kryptonite. She was also my biggest rival in this competition, and I was determined to win.

It wasn't the monetary prize I was after. It was all that came with the recognition from the premiere publicity company. I was the best, and I wanted to be perceived as such. But more than that, my cause was the one thing in this world that meant something to me. Something that needed not just money thrown at it to resolve and improve.

Lavinia opened her sleek, leather bag that seemed to double as a purse and pulled out a compact and lipstick. Then she proceeded to reapply her cherry-red lipstick.

Was she fucking kidding me right now?

Watching her gloss those plump lips was worse than being stretched on the rack. Forcing my gaze away from her, I shifted again, my dick fully erect now.

Mother fucker.

Let's see. Running code, checking firewalls in my tech security, watching fucking traffic. I thought of anything and everything to get my dick under control. Closing my eyes, I exhaled a slow, steady breath.

"Okay. Last three, you're up!" came the chipper voice of the assistant.

Damn right I was up. My blood, my dick, you name it.

I stood, allowing Lavinia to go in ahead of me, which was a mistake, because my traitorous gaze dropped to her curvy ass.

The dress she was wearing was elegantly

professional. Black, mid-calf, scoop-neck, three-quarters sleeve. And yet, the way it was tailored framed her body in utter perfection. Or distraction, on my part.

Head up, I observed the three executives on one side of the conference table and took a seat on Lavinia's left across from them. The stiff warlock made up the third contestant in our group.

The panel consisted of two men, one woman, not including the assistant settled off to the side to take notes on a tablet hooked to a flat keyboard.

"Welcome and congratulations on making it through the thousands of contestants to this semi-final round," said the thin, well-dressed man in the middle. He had the look and carriage of someone used to being in control. I knew who he was before he opened his mouth, because I'd studied every single person I knew to be involved in this contest. "I am Victor Garrison, CEO of Garrison Media.

CEO *and* warlock with Divine Seer designation. He'd made his first million at twenty-three, hit the cover of Forbes by twenty-seven and, ten years later, had catapulted his media company into a billion-dollar business headquartered in New Orleans. He'd opened offices all over the world.

"This is my Chief Operating Officer," Victor pointed to the brunette, her hair twisted neatly onto her head, "Marianne Mixon."

I knew her as well. She'd been with Garrison for the last decade and used her witch designation as an Influencer to amass a superstar client list as well as recruiting the best and the brightest employees for their company.

The only person I didn't know was the man on his left. He was a warlock like Victor. A powerful one from the signature I detected.

"And this is Richard Davis, our new Director of Marketing. Richard will be overseeing the finalists' progress till the end of the marketing campaign. We'd like to welcome you all—Willard, Livvy, and Gareth—as three of the nine semi-finalists. We've obviously reviewed your portfolios and the live presentation during the selection for semi-finalists. Today, we ask all of you to answer one simple question." He kept his hands clasped on the table, pausing for dramatic effect, no doubt, then finally asked, "Without going into detail about the cause you're proposing to adopt for the campaign, what method of marketing will you employ that will ensure you raise awareness and collect donations? Willard, you may go first."

The warlock on the end—not sure what his designation was—began in a calm and monotone voice. "I'd set up a website specifically for the campaign and use the traffic data to target ads on our specific audience."

He stopped talking abruptly without further explanation. After an awkward fifteen seconds where Victor waited for elaboration and received none, he turned his attention to Lavinia.

"Livvy, what marketing strategy would you employ?"

She straightened and began speaking, gesticulating just the exact amount needed to illustrate and attract without coming across as obnoxious. I couldn't help but stare at her, watching her expression shift with dynamic brightness. Her blue eyes widened with excitement, her husky voice inflected for emphasis, her exuberance shone like a torch in the darkness. She was in a word, bewitching.

I kept my composure, refusing to react to her magical allure. For that's what all of this was.

It had to be.

I forced myself to tune into what she was actually saying.

"This strategy may not appear lucrative, but it would include far more than local contributions for the fundraisers."

I'd caught something about local fundraising events, but that was all.

"Interesting," said Richard, leaning forward in his seat, hands on the conference table. "Please explain."

"The local fundraising event would be the

foundation of a much broader campaign using social media. I'd create our own YouTube Channel and social media profiles—Instagram, Snapchat, TikTok. I'd promote through those social media platforms, but also video live on our YouTube channel and charge donations to attend the live event online. Of course, I'd do all promotion via the SuperNet to raise awareness for the cause there."

The finalists would each have to pitch their own cause to promote, and only one cause would be selected for the final team of finalists. The cause had to be related to the supernatural world in some way. I was determined to push mine through no matter what.

"That is interesting," praised Richard, his lusty gaze telegraphing how very interesting he found Lavinia. "And what kind of fundraising event would attract that sort of online attention? What would make people pay money to see it?"

I thought we weren't supposed to share details, but this wasn't about the cause. This was about her marketing strategy.

"I'm still working on logistics and more ideas, but one event would be to video the photography sessions of a pin-up girl calendar. The models would all be supernaturals donating their time and talent for our cause."

"And you know enough models to pull this event off?" asked Victor.

"Oh, yes. I've been in a few myself and I know plenty of others who'd volunteer for this cause." She sat back confidently.

Meanwhile, I tried to channel all of my focus in preventing my blood from collecting in my cock at the thought of Lavinia modeling for a pin-up calendar.

"Sounds as if you've given this a lot of thought," said Richard.

I did *not* like the way Richard was looking at Lavinia.

Correction. I wanted to gouge his fucking eyes out of his skull with that ridiculous tie clip he was wearing.

"Thank you, Livvy," said Victor. He turned his gaze to me. "How about you, Gareth? What marketing strategy would you lean on?"

"My strength is in tech," I stated. "So my focus will be in that realm."

Not that it was a big secret that most grims were efficient in the technology department. What they didn't know was that our gift was part of our DNA. It was a by-product of having photographic memories, high IQs, and most importantly the magic-infused ability to read numbers easier than anything else. In essence, code and numbers made more sense to us than any other language.

Mind you, I wasn't complaining. I knew that I was blessed with this ability inherited from our infamous forefather who dabbled in numerology. It was his dabbling in the darker arts—the darkest, rather—that cursed many of the grims with another ability altogether. One I was thankful not to have. Unfortunately, my poor cousin Henry wasn't so lucky.

"I'll analyze the data of various social media platforms to find out where our audience gravitates. While I believe all social media has valid usage for promotion, Facebook will be where our target audience spends most of its' time."

"Why would you think that?" Lavinia asked huffily. "You don't even know our cause yet."

"True," I agreed, "however, the people with the most money gravitate toward Facebook. The average US user is 40.5 years old, which also happens to be the age range for those with higher income who aren't yet scrimping for retirement. There is every kind of business page on Facebook, many of whom are looking for a cause to support and get that tax deduction on their donations. I can analyze data, based on individual and company product purchases, to determine who would most likely support our cause. Then we target them for promotion."

Lavinia's brow pinched together. "Wouldn't that data only be available to Facebook?"

Turning away from her—because it was hard to fucking concentrate with her goddess-like features so close—I told the panel, "I have my own means."

"Are they illegal?" asked Victor. "We can't condone illegal practices."

I smiled. "I wouldn't be hacking into Facebook, if that's your concern. I have other means, legal ones, to get the information."

I'd created my own software, MIMIC, to mirror every move on FB, state by state, inside the US, and I'd been running the software for the past three months on multiple machines in my tech bunker at my home. I wasn't about to explain that to these guys.

I also wasn't going to explain that I could make a phone call to my uncle, President of Obsidian Corp., a company run and maintained entirely by grims for one sole purpose—information. Uncle Silas and I weren't close, but I was the only son of his dead brother, so he'd do me the favor.

Especially if I agreed to try to convince his son and my cousin Henry to go to work for him. I might lie and pretend to my uncle, but I wouldn't do that. What Henry chose to do with his life was his choice.

At any rate, I had multiple means of gaining the data we needed to fine-tune our marketing to the right people with the best possible outcome. But I wasn't going to tell this warlock exactly how any of that was going to happen. Either he'd trust that I was above board legally or he wouldn't.

Apparently, Victor saw something in my face that assured him I was telling the truth. He was a Seer after all.

"Thank you, Gareth." He panned his gaze to all three of us. "You've given us a great deal to consider, and we appreciate your time. We will contact you when we've made a decision." He stood and leaned over to shake Willard's hand. Then Lavinia's and mine. "Thank you all for coming."

We all stood. It looked as if *Dick* Davis was about to lean over and shake Lavinia's hand. I nudged her with a light touch in the middle of her back.

She glared over her shoulder at me, but I didn't budge.

"Move, Lavinia." I crowded her space more so she'd keep moving. Thank fuck, she did. Because her proximity was twisting my stomach into knots and jacking my libido into overdrive. I needed to get out of this room and far away from her so I could simmer down.

Once through the lobby, the three of us stood and waited by the bank of elevators. An overly cheery version of "Let It Snow" pumped out of the speakers, mocking my current volatile state.

Lavinia crossed her arms and practically vibrated

with fury. It nearly made me laugh that we were both fuming while Willard actually tapped fingers against his pants leg in time with the holiday tune.

Then Lavinia shot a hard look my way that would've terrified most men. Not me.

"Is there a problem, Lavinia?" I realized that my composure was slipping. Even the grating of my voice warned me that I was teetering on the edge here.

"Yes," she hissed. "You!"

Willard didn't even look our way, keeping his stoic diligence focused on the closed elevator doors.

"I'm never a problem," I told her. "But I'm full of solutions. For example, if something I've done has rubbed you wrong, just ignore me and you'll feel right as rain."

Just like I was so obviously able to ignore her, right?

"I think you were a little arrogant in there with your marketing strategy. And possibly lying. There's no way you can get that information without collecting it illegally."

Giving up on ignoring her, I turned to fully face her but kept my hands in my pockets, holding onto my calm veneer by a thread. She now clutched one hand in a death grip on the strap of her bag, the other propped on her voluptuous hip.

Fuck. *Ignore her hips, man!*

Time to deflect.

"I'm onto you, witch. You can't use your magic as an Influencer to win this. If you do, I'll report you to the Guild."

Her jaw dropped, and I spent an inordinate amount of energy trying not to imagine how wide her mouth could go.

"First of all, I don't need to use my magic to beat you, grim. I'm going to win on my talent alone. And second, you'd be reporting me to my own sister, dimwit, and I think I know whose side she'd take."

I already knew all this. I didn't actually believe she was illegally using her Influencer magic to persuade the judges on this thing. I also knew who her sister was. I just needed to get her attention away from the fact that I was being pushy in getting her out of that stifling office because then I'd have to admit that I didn't like the way that Director of Marketing Douchebag was salivating all over her.

The last thing I needed was this woman knowing how she obliterated my self-control within thirty seconds of being in her presence. She'd use it to her advantage in the competition to try and beat me. *Wasn't happening.*

The elevator dinged. Willard stepped in first, not exactly the gentleman. Then Lavinia went. I stayed put.

She stepped in and spun around, a frown puckering her brow when I remained outside.

"I'll take the next one," I told her evenly, finally calmer with a little space between us. "I'm not sure I could fit in there with your ego." And my ever-growing libido.

Her face and neck flushed pink with anger, cascading beneath her collar. I couldn't help imagining that creamy skin flushed with desire rather than fury.

"Good," she snapped. "I'm not sure your big head would fit in here anyway."

"Probably not," I agreed, knowing my ego was far bigger than hers but also, my other head was swollen beyond reason since the second I saw her sitting there all prim and professional in the lobby.

Her mouth fell ajar again as she got my meaning, her gaze dropping to my crotch. I simply smiled at her as the doors slid closed. Then I let my head fall back as I inhaled a deep breath.

"Thank fuck," I muttered to myself, relishing the ease in my chest when she disappeared and realizing this competition was going to be a nightmare if we were both finalists.

Knowing yet again how Destiny adored to torture me so, I knew that's exactly what was going to happen.

CHAPTER 3

~LIVVY~

I WAS on my second cup of coffee at the breakfast table, thinking about how I'd told everyone at the last Sunday dinner about Gareth Blackwater and his obscene arrogance at the semi-finalist interviews.

I mean, the man had some gall accusing me of cheating. Yes, I had the ability to use powerful persuasion magic, even implant thoughts into other people's heads, but I wouldn't do that. I wasn't a cheater, dammit!

And then, he gets all pushy, nudging me out the door and telling me to move at the end of the interview.

I had a feeling the other two panelists besides Victor Garrison wanted to be polite and shake our hands. But nooooo. Gareth cut that off and practically shoved me out the door. So rude.

"Pushy asshole."

"Who is?" asked Jules, stepping into the kitchen in her red kimono.

"That grim in the PR competition."

Jules said nothing, just eyed me before going to the coffee pot and pouring a cup.

"Don't give me that look."

"Which one? The one where I point out that you're awfully fixated on a guy who annoys you so much?"

I didn't want to confess to her what the real problem here was. But if there was anyone who would take a dirty secret to the grave, it was Jules. She was like the Fort Knox of privileged information.

She poured a little half-n-half in her cup, stirred, then made her way to the table and sat down.

"Tell me."

Blowing out a frustrated breath, I decided to go for it. "Well, can I ask you something?"

She nodded, sipping on her coffee.

"What do you usually feel when you're around grims? I mean, what darker urges do you usually get?"

"I don't. I'm a Siphon, Liv. I can block a grim's aura

pretty easily. You should be able to put up a good shield yourself though."

"Mmhmm," I nodded, picking at the frayed ends of my *Nightmare Before Christmas* nightgown with Jack and Sally kissing on Spiral Hill. This one was getting so old. I needed a new one.

Shielding was something we'd been taught when we were young witches, and because we'd all inherited powerful magic, we usually could.

"True," I added distractedly.

"But you can't with him," she stated as fact, not a question.

"Noooo," I whined. "And this guy, he makes me feel like...like..." I gestured wildly with my hands, hoping she'd fill in the blanks.

"I don't know what that means exactly, but I'm going to take a wild guess. Is it lust?"

"Ugggg! Yes, goddess help me." I pierced my messy hair with my fingers, wanting to pull it all out, I was so frustrated. "Like next level horniness, you know?"

"I didn't realize there were levels."

"There are, Jules. And let me tell you, I do not want to feel anything around this guy. He's my competition, for heaven's sake!"

My phone buzzed on the table. An email notification. From Victor Garrison!

"Omigod," I muttered.

"What is it?"

I tapped open my email and read through the email stating they'd selected the finalists sooner than planned and would like all semifinalists to meet this afternoon for the results. If we had a scheduling conflict, let them know, yada, yada, yada. But of course, they all knew we'd jump to when they called.

"They're telling us this afternoon who the finalists are. This is so much sooner than I thought it would be."

"Terrific. Well, you'll be one of them, I'm sure of it. And maybe the grim will be out."

"Yeah. One in nine chance, actually. Which aren't great odds. But I hope so," I agreed excitedly and woefully at the same time.

My emotions were all over the place. Oh! Maybe Clara could help me with this?

"Okay, gotta go. Need to pick the perfect outfit and everything."

"It's 9 a.m., Livvy," Jules called to me as I headed for the back kitchen door.

"I know! I need to hurry."

I rushed across the backyard area toward the upstairs apartment of the carriage house where Clara and Violet lived. Fred, Violet's rooster, strutted around wearing a gold tie with little black fleur-de-lys on them. I charged up the outside staircase and walked into their little den area.

Clara was sitting on the loveseat, knitting something bright pink, her coffee cup on the table.

"Morning, Livvy," she beamed, giving me and my aura a once-over. "Ooooo, something has you very excited."

"We were just notified that the finalists have been selected for the competition. So we have a meeting this afternoon. But I need your help with something."

"Okay."

She set her knitting in her lap and gave me her full attention. This was one thing I loved about Clara. She always made you feel like you were the most important person in a room. Of course, I was the only one in the room, but you know what I mean.

"So, do you think you can give me a happy spell to last the whole meeting? But also know that a grim will be there and he has a powerful aura. So I want your joy spell to counteract his so that I'm not affected by him."

"Oh, I see." She nodded thoughtfully. "The joy spell can last for hours at a time sometimes. I can give it my all. But I've never crafted my spells to compete with grim magic." She frowned. "And if he's powerful, there's a chance his aura might overtake my spell."

This wasn't what I wanted to hear, but I'd do anything. Try anything to make it through this meeting without Mr. Grinch destroying my mood. Or invading my aura space, as he so easily does.

"Let's try anyway."

"Of course," she beamed. "Come by Maybelle's before you leave and I'll take care of you."

I launched across the loveseat and gave her a tackle hug and a big, smacking kiss then headed back into the house. I hoped Clara's magic would help me fend off Gareth's aura.

Violet was making headway with her magical tattoos. I wondered if she could give me one that would block a grim's magic. I didn't have time today to see about that, but if this didn't work and if somehow we both ended up in the finals together where I'll have to spend inordinate amounts of time with this grim, then I'd go to Violet for help.

But I was feeling really optimistic. Clara was the most powerful Aura in the greater New Orleans area. If anyone could project a happy bubble around me and shield me from that asshat's lusty aura, it was her.

Yep. This was going to be a great day. I could feel it.

CHAPTER 4

~GARETH~

Angels preserve us. Have mercy.

Livvy walked into the room, and I swear by all things holy the air transformed from dull and boring to vibrant and intoxicating in a millisecond. And that goddamn dress she was wearing should be illegal.

It wasn't that it was indecent or even inappropriate. A deep, blood red—same shade as her lipstick—it covered more skin than I cared for, exposing a modest sweetheart cutout of creamy, pale flesh at the top of her chest and only a sliver of her shapely legs below the knees. *But Christ above!* The way it hugged her body, flaunting her insane, hourglass figure with overfull hips and breasts and cinched-in waist, it was unfair to the rest of the mere mortals around her.

I reined in my straying desires, knowing full well that I couldn't let her magic or drugging allure to pull me in. Instead, I turned my attention to the dais across the small reception area where we'd been told to report and waited for Victor to take his place.

Right now, the other contestants were enjoying drinks and hors d'oeuvres, socializing easily. The reception room was posh with a wall of windows overlooking the city, gilded gold in the afternoon sun.

I sipped on my bourbon neat, keeping my eye on the prize. The stage where I'd be chosen as a finalist.

It could be arrogance that told me I'd be one of the three. But I also believed in manifestation, and most grims embodied more magic than the average witch and vampire put together. There was something to be said about believing a hope or dream into reality.

When I sensed her presence right next to me, I stiffened, keeping my gaze on the stage.

"Ah," she cooed sweetly. "They're playing your song, Mr. Blackwater."

It was a slow, sultry version of "You're a Mean One, Mr. Grinch" by a female artist with a smoky voice. Doing my damnedest not to smile—because hell, that was fucking funny—I finally turned to face Lavinia.

One look at those cat-eyed baby blues, and I was rock hard all over. I pushed out a pulse of magic, hoping to block hers. The second that I did, her cat-got-the-cream smile evaporated into nothing.

"Are you alright, Lavinia?"

She blinked several times before looking away and sipping from her glass of red wine. "Perfect."

But there was a shrill note in her voice that said she wasn't at all perfect.

"You seem upset," I added, suddenly concerned for her.

Where was that coming from? I couldn't feel compassion for my rival. What was wrong with me?

She huffed out a cynical laugh. "Just something I thought would work. And it didn't."

"What's that?"

"Nothing," she bit out.

She seemed about to walk away from me when Victor, Richard, and Marianne took the stage. Victor stepped up to the podium.

"Welcome, all of you. If you're standing in this room, then you were selected as the best supernaturals in the industry of marketing in all of New Orleans. So you should give yourself a hand."

He proceeded to clap as did the dickhead and Marianne behind him. I couldn't help notice that Richard's lecherous stare had already found Livvy. It wasn't simple admiration that shone in his beady eyes, it was a hint of something dangerous. I could smell it like a bloodhound on the hunt. And I didn't like it one fucking bit.

On instinct, I shifted my body closer to Lavinia. As if I could shield her from that prick.

"I won't make you all wait any longer," continued Victor. "This was a very tight competition. As you may recall, we had you interview in groups of three. After analyzing your portfolios and interviews, we grouped you according to whom we thought you'd work with best."

I couldn't help but arch an eyebrow at Lavinia. She gave me the same surprised expression.

"Don't look at me," she snapped. "I can't help if it their grouping skills suck."

For the first time, I genuinely laughed in her presence. It seemed to surprise her as much as it did me.

"After the semi-finalist interviews," said Victor, "we realized that we had indeed paired everyone correctly."

She scoffed.

I leaned to the side, tilting my head down and whispered, "Don't worry, darling. That's a compliment to you. I'm the best of the best."

"Says you."

I regretted leaning closer, inhaling her sweet,

enticing scent. I straightened and tuned back into Victor.

"All of this is to say that we have selected the finalists according to the groups at the last interview."

Oh, for fuck's sake.

Livvy stiffened next to me.

We both knew what was coming. We were going to be finalists together, which was wonderful. And fucking awful.

"Without further ado, the team we've selected as the finalists for the Garrison PR Competition are…Gareth Blackwater, Livvy Savoie, and Willard Thompson."

A rush of elation and dread coursed through my blood, shooting a rocket of adrenaline through my body.

I'd made it to the finalists. And I'd be working with Lavinia.

Every. Single. Day.

My dream and nightmare converged into a melting pot of strange and terrifying emotions I wasn't prepared to analyze at the moment.

Everyone clapped and turned to us. Willard stepped away from the food table, chomping on a cocktail shrimp and stood next to Lavinia, giving the crowd an awkward wave.

I lifted my glass to the room then to Lavinia.

"Cheers, darling. You're stuck with me now."

She toasted me, then Victor led the room in his own toast, congratulating everyone again.

"You don't seem very happy about it," Lavinia said tightly. "Is it because you have to share the spotlight with two others? I'm sure that's difficult for you."

"I suppose you're right. I prefer to work alone."

She turned to face me, blasting me with a tsunami-sized wave of attraction. "Oh, I see. Never had a menage, have you?"

Holding onto my sanity by a thread, I replied coolly, "No."

"I'm surprised. You should give it a try, Gareth."

My name on her lips did insane things to my body.

"Why's that?" I gritted out.

"It might loosen you up. It's fun to let loose and lose control sometimes."

Holding her gaze, I attempted to not say what I wanted to say, but the devil take me, there was no way I wasn't telling her exactly where I stood on this matter.

"During sex," I said in a low voice, only for her ears, "being in control is the only way I get off."

Without a second of forethought, that image I'd fantasized more than once now popped into my mind.

Lavinia naked and bound and bending over the silk sheets of my bed. This time, I was standing over and behind her, one hand wrapped gently around her nape as I reared my other hand back and smacked her full ass. She flinched and moaned with pleasure.

Standing in front of me, Lavinia's eyes widened and her heartbeat raced to an astronomical pace. I could taste her shock and answering desire on the air, thanks to my grim DNA. That's when I realized what I'd done. I hadn't just thought it, I'd shared it.

"You're—" she cleared her raspy throat—"you're a telepath?"

Grinding my teeth together, I scolded myself for letting her know. We kept our abilities secret. It was our way. Information was the most powerful weapon of all. What people didn't know was as important as what they did.

But it wasn't this new piece of information that had a flush crawling up her neck, splashing her cheeks with pink. It was the little video I'd telepathed.

I should've said something snarky like, *even grims like to spank bad girls before they fuck them.* Anything to throw her off the scent. Anything to make her understand that what I'd sent her was a mistake, my own fantasy I hadn't meant to share with her.

But I couldn't deny it, especially seeing her reaction wasn't one of repulsion. Her dilated pupils and heated blood told me an entirely different story.

So rather than answer her question or deflect what she'd seen in my own mind, I gave her a small nod.

"Congratulations, Lavinia." I downed the rest of my bourbon in one gulp. "I suppose I'll be seeing you very soon."

Then I strode through the crowd, ignoring the well-wishers, slammed my glass on the bar, and got the fuck out of there.

As I've mentioned before, Destiny has always found me to be her favorite plaything. Seems the games were just about to begin.

JINGLE SPELLS

Timeline: Takes place almost two years following* **Witches Get Stitches.

CHAPTER 1

~NICO~

Mateo stood with hands on hips, his feet apart, squaring me off. If I didn't know where all this ultra-alpha behavior was coming from, I'd think we were about to brawl. Speaking of Alpha, his wolf kept slipping in and out of his voice.

"**I'm not sure I trust you.**" He eyed me skeptically. "I'll need to do another sweep."

"Mateo! *Please.*" Evie stood there in a sparkly blue cocktail dress, looking like a million bucks, but her husband was maniacal when it came to the triplets. "We won't even make it to the party before midnight at this rate."

He prowled my living room, circling around Violet who was sitting on the floor with the three fifteen-month-olds watching their father move around the room.

"Your daddy's crazy," Violet whispered to them.

Diego shouted, "Da!" Celine giggled. And Joaquin blinked his blue eyes thoughtfully.

"Aha!" Mateo shouted from the corner behind the couch near the bookshelves. "This is a choking hazard, Nico. It has to go." He lifted the Ficus plant and marched for the door.

"It's fake," Violet added, exasperated. This was the third thing he'd chunked onto my patio.

He slammed the door and returned, eyes roving the kitchen area which he'd checked three times already.

"Doesn't matter," he said gruffly, Alpha leaking back into his voice. "**Diego's little claws come out all the time now. He could slice it up, swallow it, and choke before you can blink**."

Diego cooed.

"**I know, son**," Mateo replied.

I remained seated on the sofa, elbows on my knees, casually watching this all play out, unable to hide my grin as Evie knelt on the floor and tousled Joaquin's curly hair. They all had a mop of curls, thanks to our side of the family. Diego's was dark, his eyes brown as well, like his father. Celine and Joaquin had strawberry blond hair with blue eyes like their mother.

"What are you smiling at? This is serious. Precious lives are at stake."

Violet had pulled Celine onto her lap, she and Evie debating what kind of witch she'd be.

"I just don't know yet," said Evie, both of them staring at the bright-eyed little girl. She was too cute for words. "They were born on the fall solstice, so she could be an Enforcer like Jules. Or maybe an Influencer like Livvy. Libras are social butterflies, and this little girl," she tapped Celine on the nose who giggled and tried to catch her mother's finger, "is definitely social."

Mateo was ignoring me now, listening to his wife, hands back on his hips. "Joaquin isn't social. They were all born on the same day."

"Well, they're not going to have identical personalities," Evie said, glancing up at Mateo and pulling Joaquin into her lap. "He's my little deep thinker. The justice-seeking side of Libra, I'd imagine."

"Now, don't get your dress all ruined before we get to the party," said Mateo, bending to take Joaquin from him. Then he promptly lifted the boy's shirt and blew a raspberry on his belly. Joaquin squirmed and laughed, the first time I'd seen him do much of anything except watch the room pensively since they'd arrived.

"Look who's talking," said Evie, standing and taking

a napkin from her clutch to wipe the drool off his starched white shirt. "That's enough stalling, Mateo. Nico and Violet are perfectly capable of babysitting for a couple of hours."

"I don't know about perfectly, but we'll do our best," said Violet, tossing me a wink over her shoulder.

Mateo glowered then Evie snapped her head around. "Shut up, Violet! You'll get him all riled again."

"So easy." Violet shook her head then walked over and took Joaquin from her. "They'll be fine. Now go before you spend your entire New Year's Eve babysitting us babysitting your hellions."

Mateo scowled but let Evie drag him to the door anyway. "If there are any problems whatsoever, *call me*," he barked before they were out the door with a slam.

"Finally!" Violet sat back down on the floor with the others. Diego stood and toddled off.

Contrary to Mateo's belief that my house wasn't childproof, I'd spent quite a bit of time doing so. Diego couldn't get up the stairs past my security gate, nor down the hall where I couldn't see him. The toddlers were confined to the kitchen and living room downstairs where we could keep an eye on them.

"Come to me, my minions!" Violet fell onto her back. Immediately Diego circled back over at high velocity, joining Celine in attacking her. Even Joaquin, the shy one, stood and clung to her bent knee.

I stood and tucked my hands in my jeans pockets, watching her laugh wickedly like a Disney villain while being mauled by the triplets. Violet laughed when Celine fell onto her belly and Diego attacked her head with an open mouth and a fist-full of hair. That boy knows what's up.

"Don't you even get that look in your eye," she told me in earnest.

"I don't know what you're talking about."

"Oh, yes you do. You've got visions of bottles and onesies spinning in that handsome head of yours."

I headed into the kitchen to get their dinner ready. "You can't tell me you don't want some adorable babies like these three."

"I never said that," she called from the living room. "I'm just not ready yet. Besides," she appeared in the kitchen with Joaquin on her hip, Celine chasing Diego in fast Frankenstein-like stomps around the table, "why would we bother when we can get our fix with these cuties then send them back." She nose-kissed Joaquin, "Right?"

He cooed as if in agreement.

"I suppose there's logic in that."

Even though the sight of Violet making weird faces and talking in baby voice had me envisioning her doing the same to a mini-me or two of our own. I unzipped the diaper bag—or in actuality the duffle bag—of items

Mateo thought we might need. I'd offered to cook something toddler-worthy, but he insisted on pre-packaging everything for us.

Celine maneuvered to stand on my feet, her chubby little fingers latching onto my jeans.

"Let's see what your daddy packed, shall we?"

"How do you know Evie didn't pack it?" Violet asked, carrying Joaquin over to one of the three booster chairs with built-in tables I'd bought for the triplets.

"Because Mateo specifically informed me that he'd cooked their favorite meals so they wouldn't feel neglected for this one single night when their parents were abandoning them in my semi-capable hands."

Violet laughed as she belted Joaquin in, his gaze tracking between me and her as if he could understand us.

That kid was whip-smart. He might have been the last one to walk, taking his first steps just a month ago, while Diego started at nine months old and Celine at a year, but his lack of motor skills didn't have anything to do with what was going on in that brain of his. You could see it when you looked at him, like he was calculating everything going on around him and storing it for later.

"If Evie hadn't practically threatened divorce, I don't think Mateo would've left them even for tonight."

My heart dropped as I froze and glanced up. "She

threatened divorce?"

Violet rolled her eyes. "She was joking. Jeesh.

Frowning, I pulled out the three plastic-ware plates with covers from the duffle bag. "Don't ever do that to me. Not even as a joke."

She walked over and scooped up Celine who was still dangling around my legs. "So sensitive," she whispered as she nuzzled my cheek and planted a kiss there.

I snatched her with my free arm, hauling her and Celine close. "Don't tease me. You know what happens if I have to punish you." I kissed her lips.

Celine grabbed my hair and tugged, so I gave her a quick kiss on the forehead too then went back to the duffle bag.

"Please tell me I'll get a spanking," she said, wandering back to the table to buckle Celine in.

Chuckling, I shook my head. "You're right. If I threaten that, you'll be packing your shit and carrying it out the door just so I'll do it harder."

She visibly shivered from here, making my wolf growl deep in my chest. No way could I start along that train of thought, because I had zero chance of getting my hands on her for several hours.

"Oh, my God! No, Diego!"

She ran over to the utility closet and hauled him out. He had a Swiffer pad, or what was left of it, dangling from his mouth and hands. Sure enough, when Violet pulled the pieces from his hands, I could see his tiny claws had sliced out.

"Dang, son," I laughed and tousled his hair as she went to lock him in his chair, "he's already showing shifting signs, he's definitely going to be a wolf to watch closely. You may have to give him his werewolf tattoo as soon as he hits puberty."

Over the past two years, Violet had done wonders for the werewolf community. Not just locally but far and abroad, giving them the control they so often lacked with the magical tattoos she and her apprentices had been inking throughout many supernatural communities.

Each of the microwave-safe plates were labeled with the babies' names. Mateo had also scrawled a note on each telling me exactly how long each should be heated and how long to let them cool before I spooned anything into their mouths. I swear, that dude was maniacal when it came to these kids. I suppose I couldn't blame him. I'd be the same.

I heated each of the plates and carried them over to the table, grabbing the baby spoons out of the duffle bag.

"How hard can it be to feed three babies?" I mumbled more to myself than Violet as I settled down next to her.

CHAPTER 2

~VIOLET~

I WAS LAUGHING SO HARD I was about to pee on myself.

Celine was giggling right along with me, strawberry curls bouncing. Nico stared at Diego, not even remotely smiling, mashed potatoes all over his face.

Let me clarify. Both Nico and Diego had mashed potatoes all over their faces. Diego's was confined to the vicinity of his mouth where he'd stuffed it in with his bare hand. Nico's was splattered from his cheek to his forehead and in his hair where Diego had launched it with perfect accuracy. Trying to share with his Uncle Nico, of course.

Diego wasn't laughing, just making these constant

happy baby moans as he shoveled the teeny tiny bites of meat loaf into his maw. They were pre-cut by their father, because of course we couldn't manage that all on our own.

Meanwhile, I took turns feeding a spoonful to Celine then to Joaquin. Celine wanted to feed herself the peas for some reason, so I was letting her. She managed to mash a few on her face and was squishing some in her fist now. She stared at her green palm then swiped her high-chair table, painting it with interest.

Joaquin was perfectly clean, watching his siblings make messes of themselves. Such a good boy. Or maybe he was already too adult for all this nonsense.

Nico went to the kitchen sink to clean off his face and hair, which left Diego open to turn his plate upside down and start gnawing on the edge.

"No, no, Diego!" I hopped up and rounded the table, but not quick enough. His canines had descended again and he'd punched holes all over the plate before I could wrestle it away from him. "Dammit, son, you're quick."

A ring tone went off on Nico's phone that I recognized as the Star Wars theme song.

"Da!" yelled Diego, bouncing excitedly in his seat.

Nico wiped his face and picked his phone up off the counter and answered it. I carried the now destroyed plate to the trash and chunked it.

"Yes, yes. They're eating now." Nico frowned and

turned back to the duffle bag on the counter. "No, I didn't see those." He rifled around in there until he pulled out another plastic container. "Fine, fine. Would you go and enjoy your night and stop bothering us? We've got it."

He set the phone down and glanced up at me standing in front of the table, then his eyes suddenly widened as he pointed.

I spun around, expecting to find Diego eating the table or something but was shocked to see his sippy cup full of milk floating away from him.

"You little minx!" I cheered, clapping for Celine. Evie had mentioned she was using her telekinesis already and to be on the lookout.

Celine squealed in delight too, holding out her hands as the cup floated closer. Then it promptly bypassed her and landed in Joaquin's waiting hands. Nico was at my side now, both of us staring down at our little broody man.

"Oh, my God," I whispered.

Joaquin blinked his blue eyes up at us, continuing to drain all his brother's milk from the cup.

"I didn't know he had telekinetic powers." Nico sat down in the empty chair and marveled at Joaquin.

"Um, I don't think Evie or Mateo know either."

"Is that supposed to happen?"

"How should I know? I've never known a supe baby from a werewolf/witch couple."

"Is he still a werewolf?" Nico asked, completely confused.

The cup popped from Joaquin's mouth then he blinked at Nico, his blue eyes rolling electric blue, a sign of his inner wolf.

"Holy shit," said Nico. "He's a werewolf and a warlock."

"Has this ever happened before? I need to call Jules."

"Damn." Nico burst out laughing as he unbuckled Joaquin from his chair. "Mateo is going to be so pissed that he missed this."

"Well, don't tell him till they get back. My sister has literally had to beg him to go out on a date."

Nico held Joaquin on his hip, looking at him curiously. "You're something else, aren't you, little man?"

He blinked sweetly like he always did. While the other two were both babbling out of their heads, Joaquin remained the calm, quiet one.

"No, Diego!" Now he was eating the table.

"I forgot. Mateo said to give him this." He reached back to the counter and handed me a container.

Popping it open, I pulled out a cleaned rib bone. "Seriously?"

Nico shrugged. "Mateo said he needs it since he's teething with his fangs."

I handed the rib bone to Diego, then fetched a wet cloth to wipe Celine's face and hands.

"I wonder what kind of warlock he is," Nico wondered, still studying Joaquin. "When do you usually know?"

"Not till they talk. Like more than the gobbledygook they speak now. Maybe around three or four? I'm sure Evie knows. She's been reading every book under the sun about raising witch and werewolf babies."

A string of peas flew through the air, hitting Nico and Joaquin. With the rib bone in his teeth like a puppy dog, Diego grinned while somehow continuing to gnaw.

Nico sighed. "Okay, bath time."

"Aren't you going to say something wise like 'how hard can it be?'"

"Watch it, smartass." He headed toward the downstairs bathroom. "Just for that, you've got Diego."

"No fair!"

Snap.

Diego now held the rib bone in two pieces, chewing on one sharpened end.

"No!" I reached over and snatched both pieces from his hands before he stabbed himself in the face with the pointy parts. Mateo (and Alpha) would kill me!

Diego winced at me taking the rib bones then his bottom lip quivered, his brown eyes widening with glassy tears shimmering on the rims.

"Don't you dare start crying. Fine! Here's another rib bone!" I shoved it in his hands, wondering how many people got to shout that at their toddler nephews. He kicked his legs excitedly and started gnawing. "Just until I can get little miss to the tub."

"Cookie?" Celine blinked at me sweetly.

"Wow. You guys are already masters of manipulation. I forgot Aunt Clara gives you cookies every second she sees you." I headed over to the walk-in pantry. "Thankfully, your Aunt Violet prepared for this."

Pulling out a box of vanilla wafers, I picked her up out of the chair and gave her one. "Just one right now, because we've got to get you all in the bathtub."

"Bababa," she answered before shoving the vanilla wafer in her mouth.

That could've meant *bath* or *thank you* or *who the fuck are you kidding, auntie, I want the whole box*. I had no idea, but I already had buckets of new respect for Evie, because this shit was hard.

CHAPTER 3

~NICO~

If I wasn't already profoundly in love with this woman, I would be now. She was on her sixth round of "Row, Row, Row Your Boat," suds in her hair, and her shirt plastered to her chest from getting soaked with all the splashing.

"Life is but a dreeeeeeaaaaam!"

Celine squealed with delight, Diego smiled while chewing on the rubber ducky I'd bought, and Joaquin frown down at the froth of bubbles in his palm like a scientist through a microscope, analyzing it for bacteria.

"O, o, o, o!" yelled Celine in the same tempo as the song.

"Oh, my God! Noooo, I'm not singing it again," Violet laughed.

"O, o, o, o!" Celine repeated, bouncing in place, sloshing water.

Pop.

Diego's head hit the back of the tub as the head of the rubber duck came off in his mouth. He splashed himself, popping bubbles on his face.

A husky laugh rumbled from Joaquin, the first tonight. Suddenly the soap levitated off the shower shelf and plopped right in front of Diego, splashing him again. Joaquin laughed harder.

"You little rascal." Violet squished his cheeks together.

Diego barely noticed, now intent on chewing the duck head into tiny bits.

"No, you don't." I reached over and pulled the head from his mouth before he choked on it. "Ow!" One of his fangs scratched my finger but didn't break the skin.

Then Diego plopped both palms in the water, splashing on Violet again. My eyes were drawn to her breasts, now completely visible through her thin T-shirt.

"Don't even think about it," she warned.

"When these little monsters are picked up, I'm going to do more than think about it."

"You're going to start wearing a condom is what you're going to do." She wiped bubbles out of Joaquin's eyes. "No, two condoms."

"You're on the pill," I reminded her.

"So was Evie!" She gestured with both hands dramatically at the soaped-up babies who had essentially flooded and soaked the bathroom.

"Okay. Time to get out." I picked up the first towel and opened it. "Hand me Joaquin first. He's the easiest."

"Good strategy." She squatted over the tub, giving me a perfect view of her ass and carefully picked him up. "I can feel your eyes on my ass. Stop it. I'm trying to focus."

"Me too."

Laughing, she carefully handed over the slippery bundle. I wrapped him up and started drying, carrying him back to the living room where Violet had spread out a blanket while I'd filled the tub.

Drying off his hair, his tight curls glued to his head, I wrapped him back up and set him on the blanket. "Here, play with this." I handed him the rubberized fire truck I'd bought at the baby store today in preparation for this event. Joaquin took it and frowned at it like he did everything else.

Taking the second towel, I opened it up. "Give me Celine."

"Got it."

We repeated the process for hellion number two. She held her arms straight out for me. I basically hugged her into the towel. Damn, she was adorable. I couldn't even imagine what Mateo would be like when she reached dating age. Hell, I'd be ready to pound any guy to dust who looked at her wrong.

As I carried her into the living room, rubbing her dry with the towel, I wondered what a daughter of ours would look like. Or our son.

Joaquin had abandoned the fire truck and was flat on his belly, naked butt exposed as he tried to grab the flowers imprinted in the blanket. Then the bee circling the flowers. I set Celine down and she immediately tipped over onto her belly and mimicked what Joaquin was doing.

"One more," I muttered, heading back to the bathroom.

"Stop, you little monster," Violet laughed, wiping off more bubbles from her face. "Mind handing me the towel first?"

Shaking my head, I let her dry off first. "Let me pick him up. He'll probably try to wiggle out of your hands and slip to the floor."

She paled, eyes widening. "Can you imagine calling Mateo from the hospital right now?"

The thought alone made me queasy. "Yeah. Let's avoid that please."

I managed to get Diego out safely who did wiggle like a worm and nearly slipped right out of my hands as predicted. I carried him back with Violet moving ahead of me. When we arrived, only Joaquin was still on the blanket. We heard the slap-slap of little feet in the kitchen.

"I'll get her," Violet sighed.

"Bring the duffle bag so we can put their pajamas on too."

Celine squealed from the kitchen then the slap-slap sped up along with raucous girl giggling.

"I'm gonna get you!" Violet chased her back into the living room, duffle bag in hand.

I caught naked Celine around the waist and tossed her in the air. That attracted Diego's attention, who then started climbing on me.

"Not yet, you two. Let's get dressed." As soon as I laid Diego on his back, I felt a stream of wet warmth hitting my forearm. "Shit, he's pissing! Give me something!"

Violet threw one of the towels, which I held over him till he was done.

"Dude. Not cool." He laughed as I took the wet wipe Violet handed over. "I just bathed you."

Diego seemed completely unruffled with my tone of voice or his own behavior. He tried to roll over and get away, but I dragged him back.

"Okay, pass over a diaper. Whatever the bigger one is." Diego and Joaquin were already a diaper size up from Celine.

"Do you even know what you're doing?" Violet had tossed me a diaper and already nearly had one on Celine.

"Yes," I answered, a little annoyed. "I practiced today."

"You did not." She let out that throaty laugh that always made me smile.

"I did."

"Then what's the problem?"

"Well, the fire log I practiced on didn't squirm away from me."

She slipped the pink pajama pants with tiny Ewoks all over them onto Celine, then started working on Joaquin.

"Diego!" I snapped, a growl rumbling in my chest. He finally stopped squirming, staring at me wide-eyed with something like recognition. Like he'd heard that voice before. I suppose I did sound a bit like Mateo, especially when my wolf was riding me. "That's right. Be still."

Finally, he was. By the time I got his pajama onesie with Darth Vader saying, *I am your father*—go figure—Violet had finished dressing Joaquin in a onesie with Luke Skywalker saying, *May the force be with you*.

She sighed heavily. "There. Are we finished yet?" She looked exhausted but was smiling all the same.

"Mama?" Celine whispered in the saddest little voice it nearly broke my heart.

"Uh oh." Violet stood and looked around. "We need entertainment."

Then my phone went off again with the Star Wars theme so I'd know it was Mateo calling me. I typically ignored my phone, but I couldn't ignore him tonight.

"Da!" yelled Diego, climbing to his feet and running around the sofa where Joaquin had disappeared.

"Watch them, please," I told Violet as I got to the phone. "Hello?"

"Just checking in," whispered Mateo, trying to sound calm, very unsuccessfully, and also obviously hiding the fact from Evie that he was calling me again.

The party was going strong in the background. One of his buddies in the art business was hosting a New Year's Eve party at his place in the upper Garden District.

"Everything's fine. You should be enjoying good food and drink and dancing with your beautiful wife."

Right then, I heard Evie's voice in the background.

"I just wanted to be sure that—"

He was cut off then Evie popped on. "Hi, Nico." She sounded like she was having a great time. "How are my sweet babies?"

"They're a handful but we're managing very well."

Violet raised an eyebrow at me, holding Celine in her lap. The baby was tugging on the strands of her lavender-tipped blond hair.

"Awesome to hear. So no one has broken a limb or set the house on fire?"

"Nope. Not one of them."

"Fabulous. You have a good night then. We'll see you around one."

"Sounds good."

We hung up. I frowned.

"What is it?" asked Violet.

"It's awfully quiet." Rounding the sofa, I found both Joaquin and Diego squatting with deep looks of concentration on their faces. "Oh, boy."

"What?"

I dropped my head back, realizing the true test of the night was about to happen.

"Looks like we've got another mess to clean up."

CHAPTER 4

~VIOLET~

AFTER THE BABIES were all changed, I had to go and change into my own pajama shorts and T-shirt, because I was soaked through from bath time. Nico and I stretched out on the floor with them. Nico was flipping through Disney Plus, then I realized what we needed.

"Hand me that remote!"

Quirking a smile at me, he tossed it over. Joaquin was laying on his back, snuggled up to him, watching the TV. I flipped till I found what I was looking for and pressed play.

The Star Wars theme music blasted through the

soundbar and the opening crawl of *A New Hope* started scrolling up the screen.

Diego bounced up and down from his sitting position, pointing both fists at the TV. "Da! Da!"

"Mum," whispered Joaquin, the first word he'd said all night.

Nico smiled over at me. "I think this is a winner. Reminds them of both parents."

"Imagine that. Sci-fi nerds that they are."

"I never in a million years would've thought Mateo would become one."

"Why's that?"

"He was always so cerebral, reading poetry and art magazines."

"Yeah, well, then he met my sister and realized he was too boring for words."

He snorted. "She did add some spice to his life."

"Ya think?" I gestured to the babies sprawled out on the blanket between us.

Celine crawled away from me toward Nico, displacing Joaquin who then crawled over Diego to lay by me. Diego was sprawled on his back, arms and legs stretched out as he stared at the screen.

The three of them watched the movie, obviously knowing certain parts, cheering in unison when Luke finally showed up on screen. But all I could do was watch the man across from me as he held Celine next to him, stroking his hand through her curls then twining a lock around one finger.

I couldn't believe it, but that first maternal tug on my ovaries exploded at the sight of Nico softly stroking little Celine. I could easily imagine what he would be like as a father, and it nearly undid me.

My heart squeezed at the sweetness of it.

Nico's gaze moved from the movie to me. "What's that look for?"

I bit my bottom lip, trying not to admit to all the sappy, nurturing, heart-wrenching feelings I was having at the moment.

Nico's gaze softened. "Let me guess," he rumbled low. "Someone is imagining babies of her own."

"Stop it," I whispered. "Don't worry. It will go away."

He chuckled. "You're a softy, Violet. Even when you pretend you're not."

Ignoring him in favor of seeing R2D2 projecting Princess Leia's hologram message, I patted Joaquin next to me. After his second yawn, and when Diego started whining, I realized it was pretty late.

"We should try to put them to sleep."

"Alright." He stood, scooping Celine in one arm, then he dipped down and hoisted Diego up in the other. "Let's get them upstairs. They won't be comfortable down here."

Nico had a king-sized bed, so he was right about that.

I lifted Joaquin to my hip and followed him. "I forgot to ask Evie what she usually does to put them to sleep."

"No worries. I have an idea."

Nico set the other two on the bed, and I pulled down the comforter so I could tuck them under. When Nico picked up his acoustic guitar he kept beside the bed—the one he used to play and sing lullabies to his niece through Facetime—my heart did another leap in my chest.

He was right. I was a softy. Especially for a man like Nico who seemed to be the Pied Piper with babies and kids. They loved him. Sure enough, as soon as he sat on the edge of the bed and started strumming the guitar, they snuggled down onto the pillows next to me and watched him, riveted. So was I.

He started singing "Somewhere Over the Rainbow" in a sweet, slow tempo and warmed me all over with his deep, raspy voice.

Celine yawned dramatically, her eyelids drooping. Diego and Joaquin yawned right after her, all three intently watching their Uncle Nico hypnotize them into dreamland. It was the sweetest and sexiest thing I'd ever seen.

As he was strumming the last few chords and

singing the last line, Joaquin finally closed his eyes, the last one of the three to give in and fall asleep. When he was done, he simply sat there, hand covering the guitar strings so they wouldn't make a sound and looking at me.

My pulse sped up at the idea of this kind of future for us. Not with dread or trepidation, but with a bright kind of joy. The kind I felt when Clara gave me a jolt of her best happy spell.

"I have something to say," I whispered.

"You do?" His brows raised in innocence, then he set the guitar carefully on the stand, shoved off his shoes and laid down sideways on top of the comforter.

"Maybe I don't want to use those condoms."

"Not even one?"

"Not a one."

"Why's that?"

"Because that right there, what I just watched, that about made my ovaries explode."

He chuckled, biting his lip to stifle his laugh when Diego squirmed and shoved a thumb into his mouth.

"I mean, I really do want kids, but I don't want to be a stay-at-home-mom. Not that there's anything wrong with it, but I've got Empress Ink to think about. And I'm still helping in the werewolf communities. The shop is really taking off and—"

"Shh." He reached over all three babies and tugged on my finger where my hand lay on top of Celine's belly. "That's okay. I could be a stay-at-home-dad."

Okay, now the butterflies were back. Full fucking force. Staging a Halo-level attack inside my belly.

"You'd want to do that?" I whispered.

"For our kids?" He lay his head on his bent arm, those soulful green eyes holding me captive, scattering my braincells and melting any resistance I had left. "In a fucking heartbeat."

My eyes felt heavy, but my heart felt full. "I love you."

"I love you too, baby."

❄

Boom, boom, boom, boom!

I shot up to the sound of heavy footfalls pounding up the staircase. Nico was up, out of the bed, and in a crouching stance before I could even blink the sleepy haze out of my eyes.

Mateo burst into the room, which somehow didn't wake the babies at all.

"What the hell, Mateo?" growled Nico.

Mateo looked suddenly guilty. "Sorry." He strode over to the bed and sat down, putting a hand on

Joaquin, the closest to him, chest heaving. "You weren't answering your phone, and I thought something had happened." His eyes were riveted on his children.

"Yeah, something happened" said Evie, entering at a much more leisurely pace, "like our rugrats exhausted the adults and they fell into a blissful sleep. I know this feeling well."

I laughed. "Y'all could've left them here overnight, you know?"

Evie gave me a have-you-lost-your-mind look. "Like that would've happened." Then she leaned over and scooped Joaquin into her arms. "How'd it go?" she whispered, pressing a kiss to the crown of his head.

"Great," said Nico. "Actually, we wondered, um..."

"**What?! Something happened, I knew it. Did Diego swallow something he shouldn't have? He does that. You just have to jam your finger down his throat and pull it out.**"

"No," said Nico calmly, looking at his cousin like he was crazy. He kind of was. "I was going to say, did you know that Joaquin was a warlock as well as a werewolf?"

Mateo's eyes shifted from gold back to brown as he stared at Evie, both of them blinking in wonder.

"It's true," I said. "He levitated a couple of things tonight. He has warlock magic in him too."

"You sure it wasn't Celine?" asked Evie, looking down at Joaquin.

"We're sure."

Evie smiled. "Well, well. My sweet little man is going to be both?" She looked back over at Mateo who'd come up behind her.

He wrapped his arms around her, brushing a hand through Joaquin's locks. "Between this and Diego being...well Diego, we'll have our hands full."

Nico leaned over and scooped sleeping Celine into his arms. "Not to mention a beautiful daughter who is going to be a knockout when she grows up."

"Nico," I warned.

Too late. Mateo's eyes rolled wolf-gold in a split second. "**I'll gut any boy who even *looks* at her**."

"Guess you'll be visiting your husband in prison then," Nico told Evie.

Evie smiled wearily. "Please don't antagonize him. He needs zero encouragement in this department."

"Couldn't help it," whispered Nico, marching downstairs to put Celine in her carseat.

"Just wait till it's your turn," said Evie, following behind him.

That warm feeling fizzed in my chest again at the thought.

Mateo had already lifted Diego into his arms,

tugging his fist away from his mouth. "Don't suck your thumb," he whispered in exasperation to his sleeping son.

I followed him out of the room toward the stairs. "Yeah. That'll mess up his teeth coming in."

"That's not what I'm worried about," grumbled Mateo. "He might bite off his own damn thumb while sleeping."

"Why don't you get him a pacifier?"

Mateo glanced over his shoulder at me like I was a fool. "He'll definitely chew that in half and choke on it in his sleep."

I remembered what he'd done to the rubber duck, which I decided to keep to myself.

"Oh, yeah. You're right."

We helped them buckle the sleeping triplets into their seats and tucked warm blankets around them.

"Thank you, sis," said Evie, giving me a big hug. "We really needed a night out together," she whispered.

"I hope he was able to have a good time, despite all the worrying and the many, many phone calls."

She looked at Mateo with love in her eyes. "I'm trying to break him slowly. You know, into letting some of his fears go. We'll be hitting you guys up again, since he'll likely trust y'all now."

"How are you doing?" I asked.

"Tired," she smiled, "but also absolutely heavenly. I

didn't know I could fall more in love with these babies when they were first born. Or their father. But I have."

We both looked over as he scowled at a tangled seatbelt latch, fixing it and latching Celine in her seat, all while being extraordinarily careful not to wake her.

"I think your husband is a little smitten too," I teased, watching him find a second blanket to tuck around Celine.

Evie snorted. "You have no idea." Then her brow pursed into a frown. "Actually, you probably do after tonight. But his love for them just makes me fall harder for Mateo, and Alpha, every single day."

"Wow," I whispered, feeling the love pouring out of her.

I wasn't like Clara who could read the emotions of people when she walked into a room, but I could at times touch the surface of emotions. Right now, the intensity of Evie's love could move mountains.

"You and Nico need to get a move on," she teased.

"Don't rush me." But my resistance had weakened to paper-thin after tonight.

With a swift hug, she picked up Celine, and the guys carried the boys out to the car. I returned upstairs, turned off the lights, and burrowed under the covers, smelling that sweet baby scent. I wish we could bottle that smell and sell it at the shop. We'd make millions.

Nico came up the stairs and entered the room in slow, measured steps, his eyes wolf-green.

"Hello, there." I sat up on my elbows, wondering what had gotten his wolf all riled.

He stood at the foot of the bed and stripped off his shirt, then his jeans and underwear, his cock jutting straight up. He took himself in hand and gave himself a nice, long stroke.

"Where did this come from?" I whispered, feeling strangely nervous for some reason.

I was Violet Savoie. I didn't get nervous. Often. Definitely not about a romp with my fine-as-fuck werewolf boyfriend.

He tilted his head, giving himself one more stroke down to the base before he released himself, pulled the covers off of me, and crawled up the bed. Like one of Pavlov's dogs, my pussy responded immediately, soaking through my panties.

His nostrils flared as he straddled my hips, his magnificent chiseled and rock-hard body towering above me. He slowly pulled my pajama shorts and panties off then tossed them aside. His eyes sparked a brighter green in the dark.

"So babysitting turns you on?"

He didn't respond more than with a tiny quirk of his lips on one side. I remained perfectly still as he slid one finger along my slit. I sucked in a breath at the divine sensation of his calloused finger circling my clit.

"Already drenched for me." All growl.

My pussy responded by becoming even more wet.

He stopped touching me and straightened, his powerful body a work of art above me. "Come here."

Immediately, I obeyed, pushing up with my hands. He trailed his fingers to the neck of my T-shirt, gripped it and ripped it in half, his gaze eating me up.

"I liked that shirt," I sassed then shut up because he started touching me.

Mounding my breasts, he pinched my nipples lightly till I whimpered at the slight pleasure-pain he induced.

His gaze held mine then he gripped me at my nape and urged me forward to his cock. Bracing my hands on his flexed thighs, I slid my mouth over the head, licking his salty masculine taste, before bobbing as far down as I could go.

"Oh, fuck, Violet."

He hissed in a breath when I sucked hard at the crown. His fingers combed into my hair, curling around my head, then he held me still and pumped his hips slowly, fucking my mouth till I was so turned on I was squirming, trying to get friction between my legs.

When I slid my hand between my legs, he pulled out of my mouth on a growl. Gripping my hips, he shoved me farther up the mattress and fell between my legs, eating my pussy on a guttural groan.

"Fuck! Nico!"

Ultra-sensitive, I tried to squirm away while at the same time fisting my hands in his hair to keep him still. He growled, fingers digging into my hips so I couldn't move, lapping and sucking at my clit with ferocious intent. Teasing my entrance with two fingertips, he circled and circled, driving me mad.

"Please, please," I begged, thrusting up.

He clamped onto my clit with his lips, tugging gently while flicking with his tongue at the very tip. It felt like I was having an out-of-body experience, the pleasure so intense, and I probably drew blood with my nails on his scalp. Then he thrust inside me with those two teasing fingers, curling them to hit my G-spot.

"Yes, yes, yes!"

Just like that, I screamed out his name and came on a blinding climax, unable to stop thrusting against his face with each erotic wave.

Before I'd fully come down, he spread my thighs wider with aggressive hands and drove his throbbing dick inside me.

He nuzzled into my hair and bit my earlobe, pistoning like mad, flesh slapping as he growled, "Another."

I clawed his back, digging my heels into his ass, and tried to match his speed, but there was no fucking way.

"You can't just tell me to come and I'll come."

He chuckled, all deep and sexy. That fucker. He braced his weight on one forearm and slid a hand between us, stroking my clit. He held my gaze, his eyes green slits, his mouth open as he grunted on two slow, deep pumps, then he sped up again.

"Come on, baby. Let me feel your pussy squeeze my cock. She loves it when I pound her like this. Mmm, I can feel her squeezing Daddy now."

"How are you doing that?" I whined, feeling the second orgasm barreling closer like a fucking bowling ball. "Why does she listen to you?"

He nuzzled into my neck and nipped me with sharp teeth then licked. "She knows who loves her, who's going to make her feel good, who's going to fuck her just right."

"Goddamn," I whispered.

"Come for Daddy."

"Stop saying that," I laughed right as I came again. *On* his fucking command!

"That's my sweet girl," he praised me, or maybe just my pussy, pulling another ripple of pleasure from me. "Yes, squeeze my dick again."

And my vagina listened to him like always, obeying whatever he wanted.

He impaled himself hard, held still and groaned as he came with hot pulses inside me. I dragged my nails down his back, which made him groan even louder.

I smiled, loving this sensation of giving him pleasure. So unusual since I used to only gain pleasure for myself with sex. But with Nico, it was different.

Everything was different. Better. Blissful. Even arguing was fun, because I knew that no matter who won, we'd be crawling in bed together at the end of the night regardless. Nothing shook this profound connection, this mating of souls, that bound us together.

Chest heaving, his dick still inside me, he lifted up and brushed my hair out of my face. Closing his eyes, he pressed a sweet, languorous kiss to my lips.

"I want to start trying for children." His wolf had retreated, his green eyes dark as a rainswept forest.

He stared at me, his expression one of hope and wonder and a touch of fear.

He was waiting for my argument that we weren't ready, that things weren't settled enough in our lives. Hell, we weren't even married yet.

"Okay," I replied softly.

Pure joy radiated from his beaming smile and bright eyes. "Okay?"

"Mmhmm," I nodded, wrapping my arms and legs around him tightly.

"*God*." He lowered his forehead to mine, closing his eyes again. "How can I keep loving you more?" he growled, almost exasperated with the fact.

I kissed his pretty mouth and whispered, "When you figure it out, let me know. Because I have the same problem."

He kissed me with long, soft, teasing brushes of his lips. The kind of kisses that melt you down to your bones. The kind that prove to your heart that it is loved and cherished.

"We should start right now," he finally said, still kissing me between breaths.

"I have to stop taking the pill first. And we just did if you hadn't noticed."

"Practice makes perfect." He pulled out all the way to the tip—his dick fully hard again—then pumped back in slowly. Damn werewolves.

He was caressing, massaging, waking my pussy back up before she went to sleep.

I sighed heavily. "Fine. If you must, then just *give me* another orgasm," I said with a hefty dose of sarcasm, flinging my arms wide on the bed.

"You just lay back and enjoy the ride, baby. I'll do all the work."

"This is why I love you."

"You love me for more reasons than that." He

continued his slow, teasing pumps. And of course, it was working, turning me on again.

"Yes, but hot sex is like in the top five."

"Good to know." He slid his palm over one breast, mounding gently in tempo with his steady thrusts. "But I think *great dad* is going to be number one on the list."

I cupped his handsome face and said in a choking whisper with all sincerity, "I think you're right."

We settled into "practicing" one more time then snuggled spoon-fashion while Nico whispered lovely words about the beautiful daughter who would look like me and he couldn't wait to hold.

And impossibly, wonderingly, I loved him even more.

❄

THANK you so much for reading! I had way too much fun writing these short stories for the Savoie sisters, their men and the extended Savoie family. If you haven't given the other STAY A SPELL books a try, check them out below.

If you'd like all the news on Juliette's new releases, sign up for her newsletter HERE.

Evie has always obeyed the house rules of her coven —no werewolves. Until Mateo comes along. What Evie doesn't know is that Mateo's wolf has a mind of his own. **And now that she's in his sights, he wants only one thing. Her.**

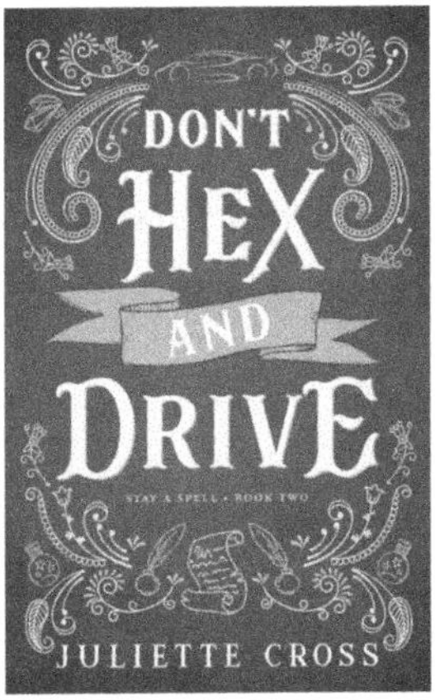

Content to remain in the background of the Savoie sister shenanigans, Isadora never saw the flirty, charming Devraj coming. Between a Bollywood marathon, supernatural dating app, secret package, and sexy driving instruction, Isadora is in over her head. **And Devraj? After just one taste, he's playing for keeps.**

Nico has been patient for far too long. He's ready to play dirty to get his mate. But when another pack shows up, sniffing around Violet…**no charm or spell can keep his wolf at bay.**

❄

Would you like to check out Juliette's backlist? Details on her website.

CPSIA information can be obtained
at www.ICGtesting.com
Printed in the USA
BVHW041150121121
621500BV00017B/271

9 781087 980669